THE GUNSMITH
219
THE BROTHEL INSPECTOR

J. R. ROBERTS

JOVE BOOKS, NEW YORK

This is a work of fiction. Names, characters, places, and incidents are either the product of the author's imagination or are used fictitiously, and any resemblance to actual persons, living or dead, business establishments, events, or locales is entirely coincidental.

THE BROTHEL INSPECTOR

A Jove Book / published by arrangement with
the author

PRINTING HISTORY
Jove edition / March 2000

The Penguin Putnam Inc. World Wide Web site address is
http://www.penguinputnam.com

ISBN: 0-515-12771-X

A JOVE BOOK®
Jove Books are published by The Berkley Publishing Group,
a division of Penguin Putnam Inc.,
375 Hudson Street, New York, New York 10014.
JOVE and the "J" design
are trademarks belonging to Penguin Putnam Inc.

PRINTED IN THE UNITED STATES OF AMERICA

10 9 8 7 6 5 4 3 2 1

THE GUNSMITH

219

THE BROTHEL INSPECTOR

ONE

Jacob Webster was a brothel inspector.

As far as he knew this was a profession that was particular to the state of Missouri. At least, he'd never heard of any other brothel inspectors anywhere else. In fact, he'd never met any from Missouri, either. Sometimes he thought he was the only one. Webster was born in England, had come to America as a young man, seeking fame and fortune. He had never expected, at age fifty-five, that he would be working in Missouri as a brothel inspector.

St. Louis was the largest city he had been assigned, and everytime he went there people recognized him. The people running the bordellos, working in them, and the men who drank in the saloons in the surrounding areas.

The saloons . . .

Drinking in one of these saloons was an experience. The men who recognized him immediately surrounded him, slapped him on the back, bought him drinks and asked him about his "experiences" since they last saw him.

"What a great job," they'd say.

"When are you retiring?" they'd ask, because *they* wanted the job.

He didn't think they'd ever believe him if he told them how sad his job made him. The conditions of most of the

1

bordellos, and the women working there, were sad. A lot of them didn't want to work there, they were forced by their situation to do so. Some of them were even being forced for other reasons, but that was not part of his job. He was supposed to report on conditions of the buildings, whether or not they were safe, or whether or not the businesses were being run properly, not on the mental or physical conditions of the girls. He was not a medical man.

He did, from time to time, see bordellos that seemed perfect. The buildings were in excellent condition, the furnishings were expensive—and so were the girls . . . expensive and beautiful—but these were high-class operations, extremely costly, that catered to a wealthy clientele. Still, even in these places he would see sadness—sometimes in the eyes of the customers, who were there seeking something they could not find at home with their wives, or who were to busy in their businesses to seek out legitimate relationships with women. Sometimes in the eyes of the women, some of whom were young and just starting out, some of whom were older, didn't have long to be in the business, and wondered what else they could do with themselves. "Old whores" were the worst—the ones who were not smart enough to move on into positions as madams, either working for someone else or running their own businesses. The dreams of young whores, who thought they might meet a wealthy man who would want to "keep" them in high style, was often awakened in the older whores, who had no other way out to even consider. They were the saddest of all.

But of all the women Jacob Webster had encountered in his work, none had ever affected him the way Jennifer Stover did.

TWO

Clint Adams was in St. Louis for one reason—relaxation. He could count on the fingers of one hand the times he had gone somewhere for "relaxation" and actually gotten to relax.

However, the last three days had gone exactly as planned. He had arrived and registered in a hotel downtown, near Market Street. The hotel was called the Beekman, and was one of the best, if not the best in the city. It also had a private livery. He was glad, as he had ridden Duke into town and could be quite sure that he'd be well taken care of there.

As for himself, he had met a woman that first evening, and had been well taken care of by her, and had been taking very good care of her, since.

"Do you think I'm loose?" Carla Moran asked on the morning of Clint's fourth day in St. Louis.

"Why would I?"

"Because I went to bed with you the first night we met."

"And every night since," he said. "Don't forget that."

"Yes, but it's the *first* night that might lead you to think I was loose."

"Are you loose?"

"No! But I'm concerned you'll think so."

He rolled over onto his right side and looked at her. She was lying on her back, the sheet pulled up to her neck. It molded itself to her large breasts, the nipples of which were making little hills in it, on top of the big hills.

"Well, if you're worried about that," he said, "maybe you should withhold your favors from me for the rest of my stay."

Now she rolled over to face him, remaining under the sheet.

"And how much longer will that be?"

"I'm not sure," he said. "I guess that depends on whether or not you keep sleeping with me."

"And if I don't?"

"I'll leave today," he said. "What would be the point of staying?"

"And if I do?"

"I'll stay . . . longer."

"How much longer?"

He frowned, made a show of considering the question, then said, "I don't have any idea. When it's time to leave, I'll know it."

She outlined his mouth with the index fingers of her right hand.

"Well then, I don't have any time to play feminine games, do I?"

"No, you don't."

"Which is why I went to bed with you that first night, in the first place," she explained.

"Which makes you smart," he said, "and not a loose women."

She moved closer to him and he spread his arms so she could mold her naked body to his, both of them still under the sheet. Between them his penis made its presence very known.

"I'm glad we got that settled," he said.

•   •   •

They woke up later in each other's arms, her big breasts pressed tightly to him, their still damp bodies stuck together.

"Ready to get up?" he asked.

"Mmmm," she said, and reached down between his legs to touch him. She stroked him until he was erect, and then said, "No. I'm hungry."

"That's what I had in mind," he said. "Breakfast."

She laughed softly and said, "That's not what I had in mind."

She slipped beneath the sheet and slithered down until she was nose to tip with his penis. He felt her tongue playing around the head, then along the sensitive underside, until she finally engulfed. The heat of her mouth was like a furnace, and she cupped his testicles with one hand while she stroked his thighs and belly with the other. Her head began to move as she sucked him. He thought he'd last longer since they'd had sex several times during the night, but before long she had him ready to explode . . . and he did . . .

"Now can we have breakfast?" he asked, a little while later.

"Sure," she said, "now I'm hungry for real food."

They got dressed, trying not to watch each other, because then they would have just ended up back in bed.

Carla Moran was in her early thirties, a full-bodied woman with a lusty appetite for sex, and for life. They'd met at the St. Louis Zoo, in Forest Park, where Carla said she had gone "To get a look at the animals—but I ended up finding one of my own."

Clint, too, had gone there just for a day of looking at the animals, but as soon as he saw Carla he couldn't take his eyes off of her. As is often the case with him when he sees a woman he's attracted to they ended up running into each other a few times during the day. He wasn't following her, but as their paths continued to cross she finally turned and asked him point blank, "Are you following me?"

"What if I say no?"

She smiled and said, "Well, then, I guess I'm just going to be very disappointed tonight."

"I wouldn't want to disappoint a lady," he said, "so whether I was following you or not, I'll say yes."

"I'm finished here at the zoo," she said. "I have a better place you can follow me to." It was his turn to smile and he said, "Why don't we just go there together?"

"What a wonderful idea!"

THREE

They had breakfast together—as they had the previous two mornings—and then she went off to her job, which she would not tell him about.

"I'll save that for another time," she'd told him, the first time he asked. "Maybe when you seem like you're losing interest."

It occurred to him that first day to follow her to satisfy his curiosity, but he decided not to do that.

He walked her to the doors of the hotel and watched her get into a cab. She had long hair that hung past her shoulders, and it was possibly the blackest he had ever seen. In fact, the only hair he had seen recently that was blacker had been between her legs. There was a lot of it there, and he found that he liked it.

Once she was gone he was on his own again—and again this was what had happened the past two days. He'd spent those two days walking around the city, and there was still plenty for him to see.

"Walking some more today, Mr. Adams?" the doorman asked.

"I thought I might, Sid."

The doorman, a man in his late twenties with the build

of a boxer, shook his head and said, "You sure must wanna see a lot of our city."

"That's all I want to do, Sid," Clint said, "just walk around and see the city."

"Well, sir," Sid said, looking off in the direction that Carla's cab had just gone, "that's not *all* you been wantin' to do, is it?"

Clint laughed and said, "You're right about that."

"I tell you what," Sid said. "I can tell you a good place to get a drink, if you've got a mind to."

"Oh, I think at some point during the day I'll have a mind to, Sid," Clint said.

"You just go down to second street, right on Laclede's Landing, and trying the Morgan Saloon."

"Morgan?"

"Fella's last name," Sid said. "He couldn't think of a better name for his place, so he named it after himself."

"Why not?" Clint said. "It's his place, he can pretty much name it whatever he wants."

"You go down there and tell me if the beer ain't the coldest you've had in a long time."

"I'll do that, Sid."

"And if you're down there around six o'clock tonight, maybe I'll buy you one."

"If it's as cold as you say," Clint said, "I'll be the one buying."

"It's a deal."

FOUR

Lately, Jacob Webster didn't want men to buy him drinks and tell him what a great job he had. Things had changed since he first saw Jennifer Stover.

It was only days ago that he had gone to the St. Louis Brothel Company to inspect their premises.

The madam at the Brothel Company was a woman named Bertha Shaw, and she greeted him with open arms—arms so fat they jiggled as she spread them magnanimously.

"Jacob, my old friend," she cried. "Come to check us out again, huh? What's it been, two months?"

"Three," Jacob said. He looked to the left into the sitting room where the girls waited for their customers. There were half a dozen girls in there right now, all sizes, shapes and colors.

Bertha saw where he was looking and asked, "Want to sample a girl this time, Jacob?"

"What?' Jacob asked. "No, not this time."

"Not this time," Bertha said, "or last time, or the time before that. What's wrong, Jake? My girls ain't good enough for you?"

"It's Jacob," he said, "and that's not it at all. I'd like to start downstairs, please, and then upstairs."

Bertha sighed and said, "Of course. That'll give me time to get my girls out of their rooms upstairs."

"Are they working?" he asked.

"This early?" she lied. "Of course not. Dolly, come over here and take our friend Jacob to the kitchen, huh? Show him whatever he wants to see."

Dolly was Bertha's oldest girl, in terms of age and time of service. She was a big, blowsy blonde with loose breasts, and at that moment her robe was hanging open to show them off.

"No, not that," Bertha said. "Close your robe. Jacob ain't interested in that. Just show him whatever rooms he wants to see."

"Okay, Bertha," Dolly said. "This way, handsome." She called all men "handsome."

"And tie that robe shut, Dolly!" Bertha called. "We don't wanna be givin' free looks to a man who ain't interested."

"Yeah, yeah, Bertha," Dolly said, tying her robe tightly. "Come on, this way, honey."

She called all men "honey," too.

Upstairs Jennifer Stover was seeing to the needs of a man named Eric Pemberton. Pemberton was a member of the prosperous Pemberton family who lived in the wealthy section of the city overlooking Forest Park. Since the St. Louis Brothel Company was considered the high-class brothel in the city, it was only natural that the young Mr. Pemberton would choose to frequent it.

Only twenty, Pemberton had been visiting the brothel with increasing regularity since the first time his father had taken him there on his sixteenth birthday. It was only, however, after he turned twenty several months ago and came into an inheritance that he had been able to visit the establishment every week.

And since the arrival of nineteen-year-old Jennifer two months earlier she was the only girl Pemberton wanted anything to do with.

At the moment he was kneeling between her widespread legs, slamming himself into her as hard as he could, crying out each time and deluding himself that she was enjoying herself as much as he was.

On her back Jennifer looked up at Pemberton. He was handsome of face and figure, and yet his touch did nothing for her. Each time he visited—since that first time—he professed his love for her and his desire to take her away from this life. Jennifer was fairly new to the life of a whore, and while she did not like it she was not sure she wanted to leave it for the likes of an Eric Pemberton. Even now he had so little regard for her, his eyes tightly closed while he desperately sought his own pleasure. She knew that's what she was there for, for men to find their own pleasure with her body, but afterward he would profess his love, tell her how wealthy his family was—and what of that? How would his a family have felt if he brought home a whore? Or was his plan not to marry her, but to simply keep her somewhere out of sight?

She wasn't sure she really wanted to know.

Jacob Webster finished inspecting the downstairs, Dotty staying with him every step of the way. At fifty-five, Webster knew he was far from attractive enough to appeal to a whore, and yet Dolly stayed very close to him, often pressed against him with her big, loose breasts, the robe gaping every now and then to reveal them. It was a game to her, though, and it had happened before. He had turned down so many "free" whores that perhaps it had become a game to them to see which of them would finally entice him into bed.

None of these, he thought. None of the ones he had seen so far.

But, up to this point, he had not yet seen Jennifer.

Somehow, in clearing out the upstairs so that the brothel inspector would not see any of her girls in action, Bertha had forgotten about Jennifer and young Eric Pemberton.

"Is the upstairs empty?" Webster asked.

"Go on up, Mr. Inspector," Bertha told him. "Make it quick, we do have to get ready for business."

Webster looked at her, and then at Dolly, who was almost plastered up against his back.

"I think I can do this alone," he said.

Bertha looked at Dolly and said, "Go on back into the sitting room, Dolly. The man wants to go on his own."

Dolly pouted, blew Webster a kiss and withdrew.

"I shouldn't be long," Webster said, and started up the steps.

Bertha went into the sitting room to make sure all of the girls were there. When she looked around she frowned and said, aloud, "Now where did Jennifer get to?"

FIVE

When he found the passageway Webster could not believe how stupid he'd been in the past. He'd probably inspected these premises half a dozen times in the past year, and he had never found it before. He probably would not have found it this time if someone hadn't been careless. A bit of cloth had gotten caught in the door, and as he poked at it the secret door opened, revealing the passageway.

Near as he could figure the passage ran along the wall between some of the rooms. He had no doubt that he'd find sliding panels to some of the rooms, panels which would give someone access to the pockets of customers' pants as they lay tossed over a chair, or dropped to the floor. Obviously, the St. Louis Brothel Company was not so high-classed that it didn't have to resort to picking the pockets of its customers.

The sliding panels in the walls had to be well hidden inside the rooms. Hell, he'd been in those rooms many times and he'd been fooled. God, how Bertha and her girls must have laughed themselves silly every time he left. Well, he was going to have the last laugh, now.

What he needed to do first, though, was to make sure these panels in the walls were really what he thought they were. He couldn't imagine what else they might be, but he

13

wouldn't be doing his job if he didn't check.

He stopped by one and, assured by Bertha that all the rooms were empty, he opened it. Bertha had either been wrong, or lied, because this room was not empty. There was a wooden chair pushed up against the panel, with a pair of trousers in the seat, but he was still able to see the two people on the bed. The man was on top, rutting and grunting, while the girl lay beneath him with her face turned toward Webster who, when he saw it, simply froze.

This was the most beautiful face he had ever seen. Something happened to him in that moment when he first saw her, and for the next ten minutes he was unable to close the panel. When the man finished and rolled off of her he could see the girl more clearly. She was young, probably not yet twenty, and her skin was flawless. She sat up and before she covered herself with the sheet he saw that her body was slender, small breasts showing pink nipples.

The man stood up and he, himself, looked barely twenty. He walked right to the chair to pick up his pants, and never saw Webster staring out the panel. He turned his back to Webster, showing a flat bare butt as he stepped into his trousers and spoke to the girl.

"I can get you out of here, you know," he said.

The girl turned toward him, still holding the sheet against her.

"You tell me that every time, Eric."

"And you haven't given me an answer yet, Jennifer."

Jennifer. Now he knew her name!

"I . . . don't have an answer yet," she said.

"I can wait," the man said, looking around for his shirt. Webster noticed that it was an expensive shirt. "But I can't wait forever."

"I know."

"I been coming here two months already."

"I know, Eric."

The man buttoned his shirt, then found his socks and

boots. He sat on the chair, finally obliterating Webster's view of the girl.

"I'll need an answer next week, Jen."

"All right."

"I'll ask one more time, and then I'm finished."

"I understand."

He stood up, fully dressed, and ran his hands through his hair.

"My family is the wealthiest in St. Louis."

"You've told me that."

"Well, just in case you forgot."

"I didn't."

"Well . . ." the young man said, again. There was an awkward moment between the man and woman—a boy and a girl, actually—and then he said, "Well," again, followed by, "I have to be going."

"A-all right."

"I'll see you on Monday, after the weekend."

"All right, Eric."

The young man paused, then walked to the door and went out. The young women threw herself onto her back and tossed the sheet off of her. Webster could see her body in profile, now. Her young breasts were small, but firm, with no sag as she lay on her back. She was young enough to be his daughter—his granddaughter, even—and yet he could not help but stare at her.

She turned her head toward him, then, and just for a moment he felt sure their eyes met and she saw him. He hurriedly closed the panel, as quietly as he could, and crept back along the passageway. He stepped out into the hall and closed the secret door.

He went downstairs and never said a word to Bertha about the passage.

Eric Pemberton crossed the street and entered the small café where Cain Barrett, his bodyguard, sat at the window with a cup of coffee. This was where Cain waited every time

Eric came to the St. Louis Brothel Company.

He entered and sat at the table with Cain, who poured him a cup of coffee, as he always did.

"So? What did she say this time?" the larger, older man answered. He wasn't older by much, though, probably six or seven years, but in terms of experience Cain was well beyond Eric Pemberton. For one thing he'd already killed several men—one in direct defense of Eric several years earlier. Eric had a way of rubbing men the wrong way.

"No answer, yet." Eric ignored the coffee. "I don't understand it. Why does she even hesitate? I can set her up in style."

"How many more chances are you gonna give her, boy?" Cain asked.

"One," Eric said, looking at Cain, "just one more."

SIX

Now Jacob Webster sat in the Morgan Street Saloon, slumped over a beer, wondering what the hell had happened to him. All of a sudden, in the blink of an eye—a girl named Jennifer's eye—his life had changed. For one thing, he had not done his job. He had not reported the St. Louis Brothel Company to his superiors for their flagrant infraction of the law. And he could not get the beautiful face of that young girl out of his head.

When Clint entered the Morgan Street Saloon he was ready for a cold beer. The doorman had left the word "Street" out of the name of the place. The location was the intersection of Second and Morgan Streets, which was apparently what attracted Morgan, the man, to the location.

Inside was a lot cooler than outside. St. Louis tended to get a little warm as summer approached. The place was half filled, some at the bar, some sharing tables. One man was sitting alone, slumped over a beer, looking as if he had just lost his best friend.

Clint went to the bar and smiled at the bartender, who smiled back.

"The doorman at my hotel told me you have the best and coldest beer in the city," he said.

17

The man tossed a towel over his shoulder, and Clint was surprised it stayed there. The man had the narrowest shoulders he had ever seen, and a protruding adam's apple.

"Lots of hotels in St. Louis, friend," he said, "and a lot of doormen."

"The Beekman."

"Ah," the man said, "that'd be Sid."

"Right. Are you Morgan?"

"That's me, Tom Morgan," the man said, sticking out his hand.

"Clint Adams." They shook hands briefly.

"Cold beer comin' up," the bartender said.

"Sid around?" Clint asked when the man returned with his beer.

"Haven't seen him, yet. Still a few minutes before six, though," Morgan said. "He might show up."

"I told him I'd buy him one if it was as good as he said."

"And?"

Clint took a healthy swallow, then looked at the bartender and said, "Guess I owe Sid a beer."

"Glad you like it," Morgan said. "On the house, friend."

"That's nice of you."

"Figure you for two more, anyway," Morgan said. "One for you, one for Sid."

"Pretty safe bet," Clint said.

Morgan went down the bar to take care of a couple of new customers, two men who seemed to find the man sitting alone of interest.

"Hey," one of them said, nudging the other, "ain't that that brothel inspector?"

The other man looked and said, "Yeah, that's him."

"Imagine wasting that job on an old geezer like him?" the first man asked. "Man, I could use me that job. Bet you get all the free whores you want."

"I'd like me that job," the second man said.

"Get you somethin', gents?" Morgan asked.

"Two beers," the first man said.

"Comin' up."

While they waited the first man said, "Hey, Cal, you think maybe we could get him to retire? Get one of us that job?"

"Guess we could ask 'im", Cal said. "You get the damndest good ideas, Billy."

"Yeah, I do," Billy said, with a chuckle.

Morgan brought them their beers. They paid, then picked them up and walked over to where Jacob Webster was sitting.

Webster did not look up at the two men who were standing in front of his table. He continued to stare into his half a mug of lukewarm beer.

"Hey, ain't you that brothel inspector?" Billy Platt asked.

Webster didn't answer.

"He ain't answerin', Billy," Cal Murphy said.

"He needs him a cold beer, Cal," Billy said. "Go and get the man a cold beer." Billy sat down opposite Webster.

"I'm drinkin' mine," Cal complained.

"Take it with you," Billy said. "Come, can't expect the man to talk without a cold beer, can ya?"

Muttering, Cal went to the bar for a cold beer.

"Leave me alone, can't you?" Webster grumbled.

"We just want to buy you a beer, old man," Billy said. "Talk to you a little about your job?"

"I don't need a beer."

"Sure you do. That one you got there's gone warm on ya."

Cal returned and set the cold beer down by Webster's elbow, then sat down beside his friend.

"There ya go," Billy said. "Have a sip of that and then we can talk."

"I don't want a beer," Webster said, "and I don't want to talk."

"Well now," Billy said, looking at Cal, "that ain't very friendly, is it, Cal?"

"Nope," Cal said, " 'taint friendly, ay-tall."

"Friend," Billy said, "we might have to teach you some manners if you don't change your attitude and talk to us."

Webster looked up at the two men finally, slid the cold beer over to their side of the table, and said, "Get lost."

SEVEN

•

Billy looked at Cal.

"Did he just say 'get lost?'"

"That's what he said."

Billy pushed the beer back at Webster.

"We're tryin' to buy you a beer, old man, and you ain't bein' polite."

"I don't want your beer!" Webster said. This time he pushed it away so violently that it spilled onto both men's arms.

"Goddamnit!" Billy shouted, pushing his chair away from the table.

"Jesus!" Cal said, doing the same.

"Just leave me alone!"

Billy stood up, and Cal followed.

"Old man," Billy said, "you just made a big mistake. We wuz gonna give you a chance to retire and set one of us up with yer job, but now I just think we'll go ahead and retire you."

By this time Clint had seen enough, and he knew that one of the men was going to make a bad mistake, maybe both of them. He stepped in just as Billy was putting his hand on his gun.

"Hold on, fellas!" he said. "Some spilled beer isn't

21

enough cause to pull a gun on a man—especially a man who's not carrying."

Billy stared at Clint with narrowed eyes, then looked back at Webster.

"That true, old man?" he demanded. "You ain't carrying a gun?"

"Anybody can see that," Clint said.

Billy looked at Clint again, wondering what his stake was in this.

"I tell you what, Mister," he said, finally. "Why don't you give the old fella your gun, huh?"

"I can't do that."

"Why not?"

"Because," Clint said, "if I take my gun out of my holster, you won't like what happens next."

Billy and Cal both studied Clint for a few moments, wondering what to do. Cal finally looked at Billy, waiting for him to call the play.

"Mister," Billy said, "why you takin' a hand in this?"

"Because a spilled beer is a stupid reason for a man to die."

"He called it," Billy said. "We tried to be nice and he was rude, and threw beer on us."

Clint looked Billy in the eye and said, "I wasn't talking about him."

Billy's eyes flared for a moment but it was Cal who spoke next.

"Jesus, come on, Billy," he said. "This ain't worth it."

Billy studied Clint for a few moments more, finally decided he didn't like what he saw in his eyes. He backed off.

"Yeah, okay," he said to Cal. Then he looked at Webster. "Later, old man. Another time."

Webster ignored him. Cal grabbed his friend's left arm and tugged him out of the saloon.

Webster looked up at Clint then and said, "Thanks, Mister."

"No problem, friend."

Clint turned and walked back to the bar, met there by Tom Morgan, the bartender and owner.

"Do you know who that fella is?" Clint asked.

"His name's Webster," Morgan said. "He's a brothel inspector."

"A what?"

"I know," Morgan said. "Helluva job, ain't it? A brothel inspector."

"What's he do?"

"Damned if I know," Morgan said, "but every man in here would like to have his job—including those two."

Clint looked over at Webster.

"He has the job and he doesn't look very happy about it," he said. "I don't think I'd trade places with him right now."

EIGHT

Sid, the doorman, came in eventually and Clint fulfilled his promise to buy the man a beer, and also bought himself one—fulfilling Tom Morgan's prophecy. Clint asked Sid about the brothel inspector, figuring if a doorman didn't know, who would?

"Oh yeah, him," Sid said. "I seen him around. Everybody sorts envies him his job, but he don't inspect the girls, just the buildings."

"I never heard of the job before."

"Me neither, until I heard about him. Maybe it's just a St. Louis, job, or a Missouri job."

"He doesn't look real happy about it," Clint said, again.

"Well, could be he's too old for it," Sid said. "Seems to me a lot of free whores would be thrown your way, ya know? Tryin' to get a good report, an' all? Maybe he's too old for whorin'. Wouldn't that be a shame? To have a job like that and—"

"Oh, he's not that old," Clint said.

Sid, who was in his twenties, said, "He looks pretty old to me."

After he finished his beer Sid said he had to go home. He had a wife waiting for him and he only ever stopped off for one drink after work. Clint decided to stay a bit longer.

He had to admit he was intrigued by the brothel inspector's job. He was also curious as to why this man looked so sad, but he had seen what happened when the other two men approached him to try and buy him a drink. Granted, they also had something else in mind, but . . .

He turned to Morgan, the bartender, and said, "Send him a beer, tell him it's from me."

"He didn't take it from those other two."

"They started trouble," Clint said. "Just send him a beer, that's all. If he doesn't want it, bring it back."

"Okay."

About an hour earlier two girls had come in to work the floor for Morgan. He called one over, gave her the beer and told her who to take it to.

"The brothel inspector?" she asked.

"That's him."

She was a cute brunette who gave Clint a long look up and down before walking over to Webster's table, adding a saucy swish to her butt. If Clint weren't already enjoying the company of a lady this trip . . .

He watched as she approached the man's table and offered him the beer. He must have been startled by her appearance because he looked up at her quickly, wide-eyed, listened to what she had to say, then accepted the beer. Furthermore, he looked past her to where Clint was standing, raised the beer in thanks and then beckoned him over.

"It worked," Morgan said to Clint. "See if he wants to trade jobs with me."

"I'll see what I can do."

"I'll send over a beer for you, too."

"Thanks."

Clint walked over to Webster's table.

"Thank you for the beer," Webster said. "Have a seat."

"I wasn't sure you'd accept it."

"You mean those other two?" Webster asked. "I'm just

particular who I drink with, that's all. Those two were just looking for trouble. I'll thank you again for heading it off before it got . . . ugly."

The girl returned with a beer for Clint. She pressed her hip against his shoulder as she set it down, bent down low enough to show him her chubby breasts.

"Healthy girl," Clint said, as she walked away.

"I've seen 'em all shapes and sizes," Webster said.

"I guess you have."

"They told you about me?"

"About your job? Yes."

"You're Clint Adams, aren't you?"

"That's right."

"I recognized you," Webster said. "I saw you last year in Kansas City."

"Do you do inspections there, too?"

"All over Missouri."

"Most of these fellas seem to think you have a great job."

"For a younger man with no morals," he said, "it would be a great job, indeed."

"Are you from England?"

"Why, yes," Webster said. "I would have thought I'd lost my accent, by now. How did you know?"

"I've known other Englishman," Clint said, "and I've been there once."

"Cheers," Webster said, and they both drank.

"So your job is not great for you?"

"It's a job," Webster said, "but lately . . ."

"Lately what."

Webster hesitated.

"I don't mean to pry," Clint said, hurriedly. "We can just drink our drinks and go our separate ways."

"No, wait . . ." Webster said. "I could use someone to talk to . . . about it . . . but not here."

"Okay," Clint said, "why don't we have dinner together tonight? We can talk about it then."

"That sounds like a fine idea."

"I'm at the Beekman Hotel."

"I know it, of course," Webster said. "I can't afford it, but I know it."

"Why don't we meet there and eat in the dining room?" Clint suggested.

"That's a fine idea," Webster said, again. "What time?"

"Actually," Clint said, "it's late . . . how about now? We can go together."

"All right," Webster said, looking happier than at any time since Clint had arrived at the saloon, "let's go!"

NINE

Jacob Webster seemed to be a proper gentleman at all times, and was dressed in such a way that he was not out of place in the Beekman dining room. Clint had taken to wearing a jacket, but kept his holster on. Drew some looks, but the attention quickly passed.

They were shown to a table in a dining room that was only half filled with late diners. They both ordered steaks and coffee, and when they had a cup each sat back and started talking.

That is, Webster did, after they agreed to be on a first-name basis with each other.

"I find myself floundering, of late, Clint," he said, "wondering how I came to be where I am."

"I don't think that's unusual," Clint said. "We all wonder that, from time to time."

"I had such high hopes when I came to this country, but . . . look what I ended up doing."

"What did you want to do?"

"I wanted to build things," Webster said, "not inspect them."

"There's still time for that."

"No," Webster said, "that time has passed me by. Up

29

until today I was unhappy with my lot in life, but resigned to it. Now . . ."

"Something happened to change that?"

Webster stared at Clint and then nodded.

"I saw a woman."

"You met someone?"

"No," Webster said, "I didn't meet her, I just saw her—and she's more girl than woman."

"Maybe you'd better explain a little better if I'm going to understand," Clint suggested.

Webster told Clint what he had found in the St. Louis Brothel Company—which Clint had never heard of. He listened while the older man told him about seeing the girl, Jennifer, how he felt something turn inside of him, change, in the first moment that he saw her.

"Have you ever been affected by someone that way?"

"Yes," Clint said, "but only once or twice."

"It's once, for me," Webster said, "just this once. Suddenly, I knew I couldn't go on doing what I was doing but . . ."

"But what?"

"I also knew that she could not go on doing what she was doing."

At that moment the waiter came with their dinners and they stopped talking while he served.

"So what do you want to do, Jacob?" Clint asked. "Take her away from there?"

Webster hesitated, then said, "Yes, yes, I would like to take her away, but why would she go?"

"Maybe she's happy there."

"No," Webster said, "if you saw her face, you would know she was not."

"If she's not then why not go with this young man you mentioned, the one who said his family had so much money?"

"I don't know," Webster said. "I can't answer any of those questions, right now."

"Maybe you should find the answers."

"How?"

"By asking her."

"I don't even know her!"

"Introduce yourself."

"And tell her what?" he asked. "That I was peering into her room and saw that she was unhappy?"

"Sure, why not? If she is unhappy maybe she'll be glad someone saw it."

Webster cut into his steak, chewed on a piece listlessly.

"I have other problems."

"Which are?"

"My job. I could lose it if I do not report what I've found."

"But you don't want your job."

"I don't like it, but what else can I do? I have no money saved, I can't just . . . quit, just like that."

"Then how would you take this young woman away from her life?" Clint asked. "How would you change yours?"

"I don't know," Webster said. His face was lined and pale, his hair white, but still plentiful. His eyes were blue, and tortured. "I don't know," he said again.

Throughout dinner Clint made suggestions, but none seemed to catch the brothel inspector's fancy. In the end they went back to one of his first ideas.

"Perhaps I should at least speak to her," Webster said. "See if she really is as unhappy as she seems."

"Sure, why not? Maybe you're wrong, Jacob. Maybe she's not the girl you think she is. Maybe you'll find that whatever turned inside of you when you saw her will turn back again."

"I think not," Webster said. "Even if she is appalled at my suggestions, my life must still change. I think I have reached a point of no return."

"Why don't you just think about it overnight, Jacob?"

Clint said. "Go to your hotel, get some rest, take a look at the situation in the new light of tomorrow morning."

"That is sound advice," Webster said, "but I think I will need to hear it out loud. May I speak to you again about this tomorrow?"

"Of course," Clint said. "Do you want to meet somewhere?"

"Perhaps I will just come here in the morning," Webster said. "I hate to impose, but—"

"It's no imposition," Clint said. "I have nothing I have to be doing. Why don't you come by around ten? We can talk, then."

"Very well," Webster said. "I can't tell you how much I appreciate this."

"Never mind," Clint said, "just tell me what you prefer for dessert, apple or peach pie?"

TEN

After Jacob Webster left the hotel Clint went back to his room and found Carla Moran there, as if she'd never left. She was still naked, and she was still in bed.

"I'm not going to ask how you got in," he said, closing the door behind him. "I'll end up getting somebody fired."

"I've been here often enough now that it wasn't a problem," she said. "Where've you been? I've been waiting for hours."

"How any hours?"

"A few."

"Left work early?"

"I did."

"Your boss said it was okay?"

"I said it was okay."

"And you're the boss?"

She opened her mouth to answer, then thought better of it.

"That would be telling."

"Why is what you do for a living such a secret?" he asked, removing his jacket.

"A girl has to have some mystery."

He removed his gunbelt and hung it on the bedpost, then started unbuttoning his shirt. She kept the sheet up around

33

her neck while she watched him undress. He thought that her lush body would look incredible with silk sheets molded to it.

"What are you thinking about?" she asked. "I suddenly feel very naked."

"You are naked," he pointed out.

"Well, I've got goose bumps, too, the way you were looking at me."

"I was thinking about silk sheets," he said, sitting on a chair to remove his boots. "Have you ever slept on silk sheets?"

She thought a moment then said, "Not to my knowledge. Have you?"

"Once or twice," he said, "but they don't look nearly as good on me as they would on you."

He stood up and removed his pants and underwear and then approached the bed.

"Have you ever heard of a brothel inspector?" he asked.

"Now you think I'm a brothel inspector?"

He laughed and said, "No, I met somebody tonight who has that job."

"There's such a thing as a brothel inspector?"

"Apparently."

He slid under the sheets with her and she immediately pressed her warm hip against his.

"Well," she said, "I guess if we make enough noise he might want to come up here and inspect."

Clint reached for her and said, "Let's see what we can do about that."

ELEVEN

Cain Barrett entered the office of William Pemberton, Eric's father and his boss. He stood just inside the door, waiting for the man to say something. It took several minutes before Pemberton looked up. Cain stood there the whole time.

"Cain," Pemberton finally said.

"Mr. Pemberton."

"Have a seat."

Cain moved forward and sat in the only other chair in the room. This was William Pemberton's home office, and it was not a place for other people to get comfortable. In his business office, on Market Street, he had the same arrangement. He was the only man allowed to be comfortable in either of his offices.

The straightbacked chair Cain was sitting in was too small for him, and creaked beneath his weight. There was no chance of him becoming too comfortable.

"I understand Eric went to that whorehouse again, today."

"Yes, sir."

"You went with him?"

"Yes, sir," Cain said. "I go everywhere with him. That's my job."

"That's right, it is," Pemberton said. "It's also your job to report everything to me. Remember?"

"I remember, sir."

"Did he see that girl again?"

"Yes, sir."

"Make her the same offer?"

"Yes, sir."

"Stupid kid."

Cain said nothing.

"If he thinks he can bring a whore home . . ."

"Begging your pardon, sir," Cain said. "I don't think he wants to bring her home. I think he just wants to set her up somewhere—"

"If Mary Jane finds out about this she won't marry him."

"No, sir."

Mary Jane was Mary Jane Dolan, daughter of Cyrus Dolan. Pemberton and Dolan were discussing a merger that would make them the two richest men in the country. Right now Pemberton was the richest is St. Louis, and Dolan was number two. They were also the third and fourth richest men in the state. During a discussion not long ago they decided that a merger would not only make them the richest men in the state, but in the country. They decided that the marriage of twenty-year-old Eric Pemberton and twenty-three-year-old Mary Jane Dolan would symbolize that merger. The problem with that was that Eric was extremely handsome while Mary Jane was extremely plain. Mary Jane was also a prude, and if she ever found out that Eric went to that whorehouse the wedding would be off. And if she ever found out that he was keeping his own whore in an apartment somewhere, it would definitely be off.

"I can't allow that boy to ruin everything I've worked for," Pemberton said. "Do you understand, Cain?"

"Yes, sir."

"Do you?" Pemberton asked. "Do you really?"

"Yes, sir."

Pemberton took a moment to allow his words to sink in before speaking to Cain again.

"In your opinion, will that girl ever agree?"

"She'd be a fool not to, sir," Cain said. "I think she's just dangling herself under Eric's nose until she can get what she wants."

"And what's that?"

"More."

"Is she pretty?"

"About as pretty as they come, sir."

"The pretty ones are dangerous."

"Yes, sir."

"All right," Pemberton said, "here's what I want you to do. You talk to her, make sure she doesn't change her mind."

"Talk to her?"

"That's right."

"Buy her off?"

"If need be."

"Scare her?"

"If you can't buy her."

Cain and Pemberton locked eyes and remained that way for some time.

"And then what?" Cain asked.

"And then," Pemberton said, "just do what comes naturally, Cain."

Cain hesitated a moment, then said, "Yes, sir."

He stood up and started for the door, which he had closed behind him.

"Cain."

"Yes, sir?"

Pemberton leaned forward.

"If this merger does go through," he said, "it could mean a lot of money for everyone concerned."

"Even me, sir?"

"Even you," Pemberton said. "A *lot* of money. Understand?"

"I understand, sir," Cain said. "I understand very well."

"I knew you would," Pemberton said. "I knew I could count on you."

"Yes, sir."

Cain opened the door and left, once again closing the door behind him.

Cain was an ambitious and capable young man, Pemberton thought. Sometimes he wished that Cain was his son, not Eric—or, at least, that Eric was more like the other man. Oh well, you can't choose your family. He was just going to have to do the best he could with what he had.

After all, he'd already amassed a fortune doing just that.

TWELVE

Clint awoke the next morning with Carla between his legs, her avid tongue and lips working to bring him erect as well as awake. It didn't take long. She moved up on him, then, and began to roll his penis between her big breasts. It was warm there, and smooth and she worked him that way until he was almost ready to explode, and then took him in her mouth and finished him that way.

He was fully awake.

"No breakfast today?" she asked, pouting.

"I'm meeting my new friend, the brothel inspector," he explained, as he got dressed.

"Is he going to get you a discount?"

He looked at her and grinned. "No discount could get me what I can get here, Carla. You know that."

"I just thought I'd ask," she said. "What's your friend's problem?"

"He's having a crisis about his life."

"And how are you going to help him?"

"I just figure to listen to him, is all," Clint said. "I think maybe he just needs to talk it out aloud."

"That's real nice of you."

"I'm a real nice guy."

"I noticed."

"I hoped you would."

He walked to the bed and kissed her.

"Stay in the room as long as you like," he said. "Have breakfast downstairs and have them charge the room."

"No," she said.

"No?"

"I want breakfast in bed," she said, putting her hands behind her head, lifting her breasts. "You owe me that because you're leaving me."

"All right," he said. "I'll go down and arrange to have breakfast brought up to you. How's that?"

"That's fine," she said, "and make sure the boy who brings it up is real handsome and appreciative of older women."

He laughed and said, "I'll see what I can do."

"I'll wait right here."

He left without looking back at her, because he knew the sight of her would tempt him to return to the bed.

Jacob Webster didn't know what he was doing.

He'd slept fitfully during the night, seeing Jennifer's face every time he closed his eyes. And what was he doing talking to a perfect stranger about his problem? Granted, Clint Adams seemed to be a very good listener, and he was a famous—or an infamous—man . . . but he was still a stranger.

And yet, who else did he have to talk to? He had no family, and no friends. He kept to himself, did his job— or, at least, he had *done* his job, up to now.

He had wrestled with this all night, and in the light of morning he was still determined not to turn the St. Louis Brothel Company in for its infraction—not yet, anyway. Not until he met Jennifer, and spoke to her, and determined if there was anything he could do to help her.

And there it was.

Laid out in the open.

Had he ever *helped* anyone before? Just to help them? Had he ever even been in a position to help himself?

So that's what he was doing. The look on that young woman's face said she needed help, and he was going to be the one to help her. Why? She'd want to know. Did he want to sleep with her? Possess her? Take her away? Would she accept the fact that he just wanted to help her, with no other motive?

Did he accept that?

When Clint got down to the lobby he found Jacob Webster waiting for him, sitting on a lobby sofa, still looking hopelessly forlorn.

"Jacob."

"Good morning, Clint."

"How well do you know St. Louis?"

"Well enough, I suppose," Webster said. "I've been here many times."

"Then you'd know someplace we could go to get a decent breakfast, maybe someplace not as fancy as the hotel dining room?"

A smile tugged at Webster's face.

"I think I could find a place."

They went down to what Webster called "the Landing." They walked past the saloon where they had met, closed now, and continued on until they reached a small café, from the door of which one could see the Mississippi.

"Close to the water," Clint said. "Rough trade here?"

"No," Webster said, "just people who want good eating. You won't find any trouble here, Clint."

"Good," Clint said, "because I'm not looking for any."

"You sound like a smart young man."

He hadn't been called a "young man" in a long time. He wondered if Jacob Webster was older than the fifty-five or so he looked.

Inside they were greeted by a big-bellied man whose apron was just barely holding on to him.

"Welcome, gents. Best breakfast in town—why you're . . . Jacob, isn't it?" the man asked.

"That's that," Webster said. "I'm surprised you remember."

"Sure, I remember. It's been a few months, but I never forget a good customer. You and your friend grab a table and I'll bring over some coffee and then take your order." It must have been late for breakfast in this place because only a few of the tables were taken.

The man came back with a pot of coffee and two cups, poured them full and then put the pot down on the table.

"What can I get you gents?"

Webster deferred to Clint with a look.

"Steak and eggs?" Clint asked.

"Comin' right up, Mister. You ain't never tasted steak and eggs like I make. Jacob?"

"I'll have the same."

"Be back real quick."

"If the food's as good as the coffee he may have found himself another good customer."

"It's good, all right. Real good."

"How did you spend the night, Jacob?' Clint asked.

"Not well," the older man said. "Hardly slept. Every time I closed my eyes I saw that girl."

"Jennifer."

"Right."

"Have you decided what you're going to do?"

"I'm going to take your advice, Clint."

"Talk to her?"

"Yes," Webster said. "I will let her tell me if she is happy or not—if she will even talk to me."

"You could go and see her as a customer."

"No, I couldn't do that," Webster said. "I could get . . ."

"What?"

Webster laughed. "I was going to say fired, but that may happen, anyway."

"You don't have to sleep with her," Clint said. "Just go to her room with her and talk."

"Perhaps I can just wait for her outside," Webster said. "She has to come out sometime, doesn't she?"

As the man—obviously more than just a waiter, probably the owner—returned with their steaming plates Clint said, "One would think so, Jacob."

THIRTEEN

"Would you come with me?" Webster asked.

"What? Where?"

"To see Jennifer."

"Now, wait a minute—"

"In fact," Webster said, "maybe you could go in as a customer and tell her about me. You'd like her. She's very pretty, and—"

"Hold on, Jacob!" Clint said, stopping the man cold. "First of all, I don't pay for women. Never have, never will. Second, I don't mind listening to your problem and offering advice, but to get involved—"

"It would help me a lot," Webster said. "I thought we were becoming friends . . ."

"We are becoming friends, Jacob, but—"

"Then you'll do it? Not be a customer, just come with me? For moral support?"

Clint frowned, but the hopeful look on Webster's face kept him from saying what he was thinking. Instead he found himself saying, "All right, Jacob. I'll go with you."

"Now?"

Clint looked at Webster's plate. Like himself, the man was finished eating.

"Why not?" he said.

•   •   •

The brothel wasn't open for business this early, but that
wouldn't necessarily stop Cain Barrett from getting inside.
He decided to try a direct approach first. He mounted the
steps and pounded on the door. He waited a few moments,
pounded some more. Finally the door opened a crack and
a whore peered out.

"We ain't open."

"You are to me," he said, and stiff-armed the door open.

The whore staggered back as the door hit her and Cain
entered the brothel. He closed the door behind him and
looked around. There was no one in the sitting room,
and no one in the hall but him and the whore. She had
obviously been asleep. Her face was pale, devoid of color—
artificial or otherwise—and her eyes were not even completely open, yet.

"What room is Jennifer in?" he asked.

"Wha—"

Cain leaned over and took hold of the whore's throat,
one-handed. He squeezed so she couldn't get any air,
waited until some color seeped into her face, then released
his hold but kept his hand there.

"What room is Jennifer in?"

"Foooo—" she croaked, then cleared her throat and said,
"Four," in a whisper.

"Thank you," he said. He used his hold on her throat to
bring her to her feet. "Now go to your room and stay there."

He released her and she turned and ran up the stairs. Cain
watched her run up, thought she had a nice, solid ass.
Maybe he'd come back later, he thought, as he started up
the stairs . . .

"It's just down this block," Webster told Clint, who still
wasn't quite sure why he was doing this, except for the fact
that Webster seemed to desperately need someone with
him.

They walked up the steps of the building, which was a new two-story brick structure.

"The door's always locked at this time," Webster said, but for some reason Clint turned the doorknob, anyway, and the door opened. "That's odd."

Clint looked around the street, saw that it was empty, then turned back to the open door.

"Can you think of an explanation for this?" he asked.

"No," Webster said, "only if someone broke in."

"All right," Clint said, "let's go in, you behind me."

Warily, they entered the house.

Upstairs Cain found the door to number four and opened it. It wasn't locked. As he entered the room the girl on the bed stirred, her eyes opened, and then she sat up so fast the sheet fell away from her. She was naked, and her breasts were like two firm pieces of fruit. Cain had to stop and admire Eric's taste in women. This one really was a beauty.

"W-who are you?" she asked.

"A friend."

"Whose friend?"

"Yours, I hope," he said, approaching the bed. She cringed as he came closer and closer.

"You're Jennifer?" he asked.

"Yes. We're closed. W-what do you want?"

"Just to give you some advice."

"About what?"

"Eric Pemberton."

"Eric . . . ?" She stared at the man for a moment, then realized who he was. "You're Cain."

"Right."

"Eric's bodyguard."

"Right again."

"You go everywhere he goes."

"You're a smart girl."

"Is he here?"

"No, he's home," Cain said. "I just came today to give you some advice."

The door opened behind him and Bertha came in. All he saw was a fat old woman in a housedress.

"You can't come in here—"

He turned, put his big hand right against her huge breasts and shoved her back out of the room so hard she bounced off the wall in the hall. He slammed the door and turned back to Jennifer, who was very frightened now. Eric had told her that Cain killed people and felt no remorse over it.

"I want to be like that," Eric had said.

"A killer?" she asked.

"Confident."

She didn't see it as confident. What she saw now in Cain's face was the killer that he was.

FOURTEEN

Downstairs Clint and Webster heard the sound of Bertha striking the wall and bouncing off. Clint ran up the stairs in time to see the mountain of a woman struggling to get up. He went to help her, but needed Webster's assistance to finally get her to her feet.

"H-he's in there," she said, pointing to the door of room four. "You have to help her."

"That's Jennifer's room," Webster said, and lunged for the door. He bounced off, as it was locked. "Jennifer!" he shouted, and pounded on it.

"Do you have a key?" Clint asked the woman.

She nodded.

"Get it."

Clint didn't try to break the door down because there was no sound coming from the other side. No commotion, no cries for help. Webster, on the other hand, continued to bang on the door and call the girl's name.

When Bertha reappeared with the key Clint took it from her, moved Webster aside and unlocked the door. He went in first, followed by the brothel inspector and the madam.

The girl was still sitting up in bed, but was holding the sheet to her chest, now. She was breathing hard, and her eyes were wide.

"Jennifer?" Clint said. "Are you all right?"

"You poor thing!" Bertha said, bursting past Clint to the bed, where she clasped the obviously frightened girl to her bosom.

Webster, now that he saw the girl was all right, stood back and watched.

"What happened?" Clint asked.

"A man came busting in here looking for her," Bertha said. "He knocked down one of my other girls and came up here. When I tried to stop him he knocked me down."

Clint was impressed. It would take a big man to knock down this woman.

"Do you know who he was?" he asked.

"No," Bertha said, "never saw him before."

Clint became aware of the woman's skin, which was as pasty white as dough.

"Jennifer?" he said. "Did you know him?"

She just stared at him.

"What did he want?"

Stare.

"What did he say to you?"

Stare.

Clint looked over at the window, which was open. Being a modern building there was a fire escape outside, and the man had obviously used it to get out. Clint stuck his head out the window, looked around, but saw no one.

"Jennifer—"

"She can't answer any questions now," Bertha said, cutting him off. "Can't you see she's scared to death?"

"Do you want to call the law, Ma'am?" Clint asked Bertha.

At the mention of law Jennifer grabbed Bertha and held her more tightly, shaking her head.

"No," Bertha said, "no law. There's no harm done."

Right then another man came rushing into the room. He was wearing trousers but no shirt, and he had the build of an old boxer gone thick around the middle. He was obviously the house bouncer, and from the look of him he had been in bed—maybe not alone.

"What happened?" he demanded. "Who are you two—"

"Late as usual, Bubba," Bertha said. "These gentlemen just saved Jennifer, which is your job."

"I was, uh, sleepin'," the man complained. "I didn't hear nothin'."

"As usual," she said. She looked at Clint and Webster, and only then seemed to realized who Webster was.

"The inspector," she said.

"Yes."

"What brings you back here?"

He searched for an answer, then said, "Just a question or two, but they can wait for another time."

"Well, you gentlemen earned a free night in my house, anytime you want it," Bertha said, "but I got to ask you to leave now so I can calm this poor girl down."

"Yes, Ma'am," Clint said. "We'll be on our way."

"Bubba?" she said. "Would you see the men out?"

He put a hand like a ham on each of their shoulders and said, "Gents? This way out."

Cain Barrett delivered his message and made his exit by the fire escape when he heard the men in the hall. He didn't need to have this get out of hand, right now. After all, he *was* just delivering a message.

When he got to the street he immediately ducked into an alley he knew would take him through to another street, and then he headed back to the Pemberton home, satisfied that he had done his job.

When Clint and Webster were outside Clint asked, "Any idea what that was about?"

"No," Webster said, "none—but Clint, now I know that girl needs help."

"Yeah," Clint said, scratching his nose, "I think we all kind of got that message, Jacob."

FIFTEEN

Clint and Webster stopped at a saloon neither had ever been to before. It was several blocks from the brothel which, they assumed, would still be opening for business at the usual time.

"Takes a lot to keep a brothel closed," Webster said, over a beer.

"I've noticed that, over the years."

"What do you think was going on back there?"

Clint shrugged.

"Maybe an irate former customer."

"Bertha said she never saw him before," Webster said.

"Bertha?"

"The big woman," the brothel inspector said. "She's the madam, and she never forgets a face."

"How about your girl?" Clint asked.

"She's not my girl . . . but what about her?"

"She knows who the guy was."

"You think so?"

"I know so," Clint said. "Did you see how scared she was when I mentioned the law? Whoever this guy was, he warned her about calling the police."

"So what do we do?"

"Well, you still want to help her, don't you?"

"Now more than ever," Webster said.

"Then we give her a little time to recover from the experience, and then we go back and go ahead with the plan."

"You mean for me to . . . talk to her?"

"That's right."

Webster sat back and took a deep breath.

"Jacob, that's what you want."

"I know."

"You were sure in a hurry to batter down her door a little while ago, calling her name."

"I was afraid for her, then."

"And not now?"

"No—I mean, yes, I still am."

"Okay, so nurse your beer and we'll go back in a little while."

"They won't open until five."

"We want to go back just before they open," Clint said.

"They won't let us in."

"Yes, they will," Clint said. "We're the heroes of the day, remember?"

"Eric!"

Eric Pemberton stopped just short of the front door. His father's voice usually did that to him, stopped him right in his tracks. He'd been trained that way from long, long ago.

He turned and saw his father coming down the stairs from the second floor. The two men were almost identical except for the thirty years—and thirty pounds—that separated them, and the fact that the senior Pemberton's hair had gone gray.

"Where are you going?"

"Out."

"To what whorehouse?"

"No," Eric said. "I do go other places, Father."

"Where's Cain?"

"I don't know."

"Wait for him, then," Pemberton said. "I don't want you going out without him."

Ever since Eric was small his father had been expecting a kidnap attempt on him. Now that he was twenty Eric chafed under the constant supervision he received from Cain Barrett. He liked Cain, but he was also afraid of him—and very aware that the man worked for his father, and not for him.

"Father," Eric said, "I'm perfectly capable—"

"Go have a snack or something," Pemberton said, cutting his son off. "You're not to leave this house without Cain, is that understood?"

"Yes, sir."

Someone else came down the stairs and both men turned. It was Eric's sister, Alicia—the apple of her doting father's eye. It didn't seem fair, though, that Alicia didn't have a bodyguard. As much in love with his daughter as he was their father just didn't think there was any chance that kidnappers would take a daughter when they could take a son.

"Are you picking on poor Eric again, Daddy?"

"I'm just trying to keep my children safe, precious."

Eric winced at his father's pet name for his older sister.

At twenty-three Alicia Pemberton had all her mother's beauty and grace, and her father's stubborness and strength. Eric had his father's looks, but his mother's gentler nature.

Alicia approached her father and kissed his cheek.

"Eric can come out with me, Daddy," she said, making a face at her brother over her father's shoulder. "He'll be safe with me."

"Never mind, young lady," Pemberton said. "Eric will stay here and wait for Cain to come back."

At the mention of Cain's name it was Alicia who made a face. Cain had made no secret of the fact that he wanted Alicia, ever since she was sixteen. Now she was a grown woman, and the man still made her flesh crawl.

"I tried, Eric."

"Thanks." As much as their father doted on her, and as

much as he envied her freedom to come and go as she pleased, Eric loved his sister very much.

"Can I do anything for you, Daddy, while I'm out?"

"That's all right, sweetie," Pemberton said. "You just run along and buy a dress, or something."

Brother and sister exchanged a glance that spoke volumes. They both knew there was no way they would ever get their father to treat them differently. Alicia went out the door, Eric to the kitchen, and Pemberton turned and walked to his office.

SIXTEEN

Alicia Pemberton was not going out to buy a new dress. She was going to the St. Louis Brothel Company to talk to the little whore who was driving her brother to distraction. Their father was already tremendously disappointed in Eric because he didn't have the old man's ruthless streak. If Eric ruined this wedding with Mary Jane because of some whore, their father would never forgive him.

Alicia had decided that she had to save her baby brother.

As Clint and Jacob Webster left the saloon to go back to the whorehouse a young woman about twenty-two or- three walked past. They both stopped to let her go by and then stepped onto the street and looked after her. She was extremely pretty, graceful, seemed to be wearing expensive clothes.

"You don't think . . ." Clint said.

"Nah . . ." Webster said. "She's just walking in the same direction."

They started walking toward the whorehouse, the woman about a half a block in front of them. They kept pace so they wouldn't catch up to her or pass her. Clint found the sway of her hips and the play of her butt beneath her dress extremely pleasing.

Finally, when the whorehouse came into sight, the young woman went up the steps and Clint put his hand out to stop Webster.

"Let's see what happens," he said.

"I can't believe she's a whore."

"If she is," Clint said, "she's probably a very expensive one."

But instead of entering the building the girl knocked, then knocked again.

"Maybe she's going to apply for a job," Clint said. "Maybe she's bored and looking for something new."

The door opened and the girl stepped inside.

"Honey," Bertha said, looking Alicia Pemberton up and down, "if you're looking for a job you're hired. I don't even care if you have experience or not."

Alicia, rather than getting insulted, laughed and said, "I suppose I should take that as a compliment, Ma'am, but I'm not here about a job."

"Then why are you here?" the big woman asked.

"I'm here about one of your girls."

"Honey," Bertha said, "I don't know if any of my girls go that way, but I can find out—"

"No, no," Alicia said, "you still don't understand. I just want to talk to one of your girls."

"Talk?"

"That's all."

"You'd still have to pay."

"That's no problem."

Bertha looked Alicia up and down, again, looking for some sign that this young woman was trouble.

"Any girl in particular, honey?"

"Yes," Alicia said, "the one my brother likes."

"And who's your brother?"

"Eric Pemberton."

The woman stared at her for a moment.

"I know he comes here," Alicia said.

"Oh, he comes here, all right," Bertha said. "I guess I just didn't expect to ever meet his sister."

"Well, can I see her?"

"She's had kind of a scare today," Bertha said. "A big man came busting in here today and threatened her—but if you only want to talk . . ."

"That's all," Alicia said. "I swear." Then she added, "I like men."

"And I'm sure they like you back, honey," Bertha said, "which is why I'd give you a job here in a minute."

Alicia smiled and said, "No job."

"All right," Bertha said. "Wait here and I'll see if Jennifer will talk to you."

"Thank you."

As Bertha went up the stairs Alicia walked into the sitting room to take a look around. The furniture seems expensive, if somewhat . . . gaudy, and at the moment there were no girls sitting in there. Apparently, she had come just before the place was to have opened.

She heard the woman heavily descending the steps, and imagined that everything this woman did she did heavily. She wondered if the madam had ever been a whore herself, and as the woman came into sight just couldn't imagine it.

"Jennifer says she'll talk to you."

"All right."

"I got to charge you double, though."

"Double?"

Bertha nodded.

"If a man comes in looking for her, you're taking up her time," Bertha said, "talking."

"I see."

"For what I got to charge you double."

"All right," Alicia said, "double it is."

Bertha hesitated, then said, "In advance."

Alicia opened her purse and paid Bertha the amount of money she asked for without blinking an eye. Bertha tucked the money away in her mountainous cleavage.

"Okay, honey," she said, "follow me."

SEVENTEEN

Alicia followed Bertha up the stairs to the second floor just as Clint and Webster decided to mount the front steps and knock.

"They can wait," Bertha said as Alicia looked at her. "They always do."

She led her to room four, knocked on the door and opened it.

"Enjoy, is what I always tell 'em," Bertha said.

"Thank you."

Alicia entered the room and Bertha went down to answer the door.

When the door opened Clint smiled at Bertha. They may have been heroes for the morning but she didn't smile back now.

"Come back for your free roll?" she asked.

"Came back to talk to Jennifer."

"About what?"

"It's private."

She looked at him, then Webster, then him again.

"Your kind of private, or his?"

"His," Clint said.

61

"The brothel inspector?" she said. "What did she do wrong?"

"Nothing," Webster said.

"Then why do you want to talk to her?"

He hesitated, then took refuge behind "It's private" again.

Bertha leaned against the door—something the door was barely able to withstand—and eyed them for a moment.

"Well, I guess one of us owes it to you," she said, finally. "Come on in and sit down. She's busy, at the moment."

"I didn't think you were open, yet," Clint said.

"We ain't."

She had to back completely out of the doorway to allow them to pass, then step to it again to close the door.

"Then how could she be busy?" Clint asked. "We only saw a woman come in."

"Then that's how," she said. "I can't stay and entertain you. Some of the girls will be down soon, and one of them will take you up when Jennifer is available." She eyed them again. "You both gonna go up."

"No," Clint said, "just him."

She nodded, and left them to enter the sitting room.

Alicia saw the girl sitting on the bed, her hands in her lap. She was very pretty, and looked incredibly young. She was dressed for work, wearing a flimsy nightgown.

"You're Eric's sister?" she asked.

"That's right."

"What do you want?"

"Your name is Jennifer?"

"That's right."

"I just want to talk to you, Jennifer."

"That's what Bertha said. About what?"

"About my brother."

Jennifer remained silent.

"Has he made you certain offers?"

"Y-yes."

"Do you know that he's supposed to be getting married next month.?"

Jennifer blinked her eyes in genuine surprise.

"No, I didn't know that."

"Does it make a difference?"

She blinked again.

"To him or me?"

"To you?"

"I don't understand."

"Now that you know he's getting married, would you still accept his offer?" Alicia asked.

"What offer is that?"

"I didn't come here to play games."

"Do you think your brother has asked me to marry him?"

"Has he?"

"He has asked me to leave here to be taken care of by him," Jennifer said. "Marriage was never mentioned."

"So . . . he wants to keep you?"

Jennifer lifted her chin and said, "You would have to ask your brother what he wants to do."

"And do you intend to be kept by him?"

"I don't intend to be kept by any man."

Alicia gave Jennifer a disbelieving look.

"He's offering to take you out of this place," she said. "Why would you say no to him?"

"Maybe," Jennifer said, "I don't want to leave this place."

"I find that hard to believe."

"Well, you're a woman," Jennifer said. "Maybe this would be easier for you to believe. Perhaps I don't want to leave here with him."

Alicia thought that over for a moment, and then said, "Yes, I would find that easier to believe."

EIGHTEEN

From the sitting room Clint and Webster saw the young woman who had entered the house before them come down the steps and leave. Another young woman—a busty blonde in a filmy nightgown—came in and said to them, "Jennifer can see you now. Which one of you is the lucky man?"

"Him," Clint said, getting up quickly. "You go ahead up, Jacob. I'll meet you at my hotel."

"Where are you going?"

"After that girl," Clint said. "I want to talk to her."

Clint hurried past the blonde and out the door. She looked at Webster and asked, "Are you ready?"

Webster cleared his throat and said, "Ready."

When Clint got outside he looked both ways and saw the woman walking down the street to his left. He hurried down the steps and took off after her. He slowed down, not wanting to frighten her by running up to her. He maintained the same half block distance he and Webster had used before and simply followed her for a few blocks. It seemed as if she wasn't going anywhere in particular, so he decided to quicken his pace and catch up to her.

"Excuse me," he said, when he was almost right behind her.

She stopped and turned, looked at him curiously, then suspiciously.

"Yes? Can I help you?"

"I saw you, uh, back there at the house," he said. "I'd like to talk to you."

"Oh, you've made a mistake," she said, very reasonably. "I'm not one of the girls. You'll have to go back to the house and choose someone else."

"No," he said, "you don't understand. I just want to talk."

"They do that, too."

"No," he said, again, "I want to talk to you."

"I told you," Alicia said, "I'm not one of the girls."

"I know you're not."

"Oh? Wait, didn't I see you—were you following me to that house? Weren't you inside when I left?"

"Yes, to both," he said. "Actually, no to the first one."

Instead of looking curious or suspicious, she now looked amused.

"Well, which is it?"

"I was walking behind you, but not following you," he said. "We were going to the same place."

"Well," she said, "not for the same reason, I assure you."

"No, I didn't think so," he said. "Look, let me introduce myself. My name is Clint Adams and I'd like to talk to you about a girl named Jennifer."

"Jennifer . . . the whore?"

"Yes. You just talked with her yourself, didn't you?"

"What business is it of yours?"

"None, actually," he said. "I wouldn't blame you if you turned around and just kept walking, but I really would like to talk to you, just for a little while. Could we go somewhere for a cup of coffee?"

She studied him for a moment.

"I was going to say you look harmless enough," she said,

"but you don't. Still . . . I'm curious. All right, Mr. Adams. A cup of coffee, it is."

Clint looked around and didn't see a place within sight.

"I know a place nearby," she said. "Do you mind if I choose?"

"No, not at all," he said. "I don't know St. Louis very well."

"Come this way, then," she said. "It's only a few blocks away."

The busty blonde knocked on the door of room four, opened it and told Webster, "Enjoy."

"Uh, thank you."

He went into the room and she closed the door behind him.

"You're one of the men who helped me," Jennifer said.

"Yes."

"Have you come back for your free turn?"

"Oh, uh . . . no, no, I haven't . . ." he stammered.

"Then why did you come back?"

"I, uh, want to talk to you."

She frowned.

"A lot of people seem to want to talk to me today," she said. "What do you want to talk about?"

"Uh . . . your happiness?"

"Oh," she said, "I see."

"I . . . don't understand."

"You want to take me away from all this," she said, "to make me happy, is that it?"

"I, uh—"

"You think if I leave here and live with you I'll be a happy woman?" she asked.

"Uh, no . . . not at all," he said.

"Then what's this about?"

"I simply wanted to ask you if you're happy here," he said, "that's all."

"That's it?"

He nodded.

"Just the one question?"

"Yes," he said, "just the one question."

NINETEEN

Alicia Pemberton led the way to a small café that was only three blocks from where they'd been talking. There was very little conversation on the way there, save for her introducing herself by name.

When they sat down a waiter came rushing over and greeted Alicia by name—that is, "Miss Pemberton."

"Some coffee, Gregory," she said. "A pot, I think. My friend and I have some talking to do."

"Yes, Ma'am," the thirtyish, obviously smitten waiter said.

"And some pie, Gregory," Clint said. "Peach for me."

"None for me," Alicia said.

Gregory nodded and rushed off to fill their order.

"Are you used to that kind of treatment?" Clint asked.

"Does my name mean anything to you, Mr. Adams?"

"I can't say that it does, Miss Pemberton."

She frowned, studied him.

"Are you being honest with me?"

"Brutally, I'm afraid."

"You don't know that my father is the richest man in Missouri?"

"Is he?" Clint asked. "The richest? My, my . . ."

"If you didn't know that, why did you ask if I'm used to this kind of treatment?"

"I was referring to the fact," Clint said, "that you are beautiful, and that the waiter is obviously infatuated with you."

She said, "Oh," feeling very silly. "Well . . ."

"Never mind," he said. "You don't need to answer. A young woman who looks like you, you would have to be used to that treatment."

"Well . . ." she said again, this time chagrined. She decided to change the subject. "I do happen to recognize your name."

"Do you?"

"Yes," she said. "It's part of the reason I agreed to have coffee with you. It's not every day I get to meet a Western legend."

"Oh," he said, "that."

"You're not happy with being recognized for who you are?"

"For who I am, yes," he said. "Not for who people think I am."

"You mean you're not the Gunsmith?"

"That's just a label somebody slapped on me years ago and it's stuck. As far as I'm concerned, I'm Clint Adams."

"I see."

"Do you?"

"Yes," she said, "I actually understand that. See, nobody ever sees me for who I am. As you pointed out, they see me for my looks—or as I was pointing out, as my father's daughter."

"So, it seems we're in the same boat, then."

"It would seem so," she said, "to a certain degree."

Gregory returned then with a pot of coffee, two cups, and Clint's peach pie.

"Anything else, Ma'am?"

"No, Gregory, thank you."

He left, disappointed that he could not do more for her.

"Maybe we're wrong," Clint said.

"About what?" She picked up a spare fork from the table and held it poised over his pie. "May I?"

"Of course."

"Wrong about what?" she asked again, breaking off just a small piece of pie with the tip of her fork.

"About Gregory," Clint said. "Maybe he likes you because you remember his name."

"Hmm," she said, "somehow I don't think that's the case, but it was a nice thought."

He cut a piece of pie and ate it, then pushed it across to her. This time she took a bigger piece.

"Maybe we should get onto what you wanted to talk to me about," Alicia said. "The whore? Jennifer?"

"My friend—the man I was with when you saw me— has it in his mind that the girl needs help."

"What kind of help?"

"Hopefully," Clint said, "that's what he's finding out right now."

"Why did you want to talk to me, then?"

"To see if you knew anything about her."

"I know very little about her," Alicia said. "In fact, I never met her until today."

"Really? Then why were you there to see her?"

Alicia finished the last bit of Clint's pie—he'd had only one bite—and took her time swallowing it, then washing it down with some coffee.

"I'm not at all sure that's any of your business," she said, finally.

"You're probably right," he said. "I'm really just asking out of curiosity—which is the same reason you're here, isn't it?"

"You have a point."

He waited to see what else she was going to say, but she just sat there silently.

"Well?" he asked.

"I'm thinking," she said.

While she thought Clint filled their coffee cups and then signalled to the waiter to bring another pot. By the time it arrived Alicia didn't exactly know why, but she decided to tell Clint why she was at the St. Louis Brothel Company.

TWENTY

"Sounds like your brother is a little intimidated by your father," Clint said, when she was done.

"And who isn't?"

"Are you?"

"Me? There's no reason for me to be intimidated. He doesn't expect anything from me except to be pretty. I'm his little girl, I'm just a daughter. Eric, on the other hand, is . . . a son!" She said it very dramatically.

"How do you feel about that?" he asked.

"The way he treats me? Or Eric?"

"Both."

"I don't blame Eric for what my father does, if that's what you mean. We're very close, which is why I was trying to do him a favor this afternoon."

"And that was?"

"I was trying to keep him from ruining his future. If he succeeds in getting that whore to let him keep her my father will be livid. If he ruins that merger, my father will kill him."

"Not literally."

"What? No, of course not, but he'll make his life a living hell, and just might disown him."

"And what did the girl have to say?"

"Well, actually, she kind of put my mind at ease. She said she didn't want to go with Eric."

"And you believed her?"

"Yes."

"Why do you think she won't go with him? Is she happy where she is?" he asked.

"She's not happy being a whore," Alicia said.

"Did she say that?"

"She didn't have to. I'm a woman, I can see these things. As to why she won't go with him the answer is very simple—she doesn't like him."

"And that doesn't bother you?"

"That a whore doesn't like my brother? No, that doesn't bother me in the least."

"So now you can go back and tell you father—"

"Whoa, slow down," she said, putting her hands out. "My father didn't send me there today. This was my idea."

"I didn't mean to imply that you were 'sent,' " he said, apologetically. "But you can certainly put your father's mind at ease about it."

"If my father knew I went to a whorehouse," she said, "he would kill *me—literally*."

"I see."

"Eric will find out her answer next week, when he goes to see her," she said. "That's good enough for me."

"And what about Mary Jane?"

"What about her?"

"How would she feel about all this?"

"I don't know Mary Jane very well," she said. "Actually, just well enough to dislike her."

"Why's that?"

"Because for a girl who is as plain looking as she is she's very arrogant," Alicia said.

"Maybe she's just confident?"

"She's dumb," Alicia said, "as a stump, and Eric could do so much better for himself."

"But not better for your father, huh?"

"This marriage is perfect for my father," she said. "He'd do anything to make sure it happens."

"Wait a minute," Clint said, "would he send a man to threaten the girl? Or frighten her?"

"He might," Alicia said. "In fact, I know just the man he would send. Did that happen? Is that what that fat woman meant when she said something had happened to that whore today?"

"The whore's name is Jennifer," Clint said, "and yes, a man broke into her room today and threatened her."

"What did he say? What did he look like?"

"She's too frightened to say."

Alicia looked down at the table top.

"It must have been Cain."

"Cain?"

"Cain Barrett," she said, looking at Clint. "He's been my brother's bodyguard since Eric was sixteen. He has a reputation for having killed some men before, and since, coming to work for my father."

"What does he look like?"

"He's a big man," she said, "and formidable looking."

"Young? Old?

"Oh, he's young, about twenty-five or -six."

"How old is Eric?"

"Twenty."

"So Cain's been around four years."

"That's right."

"And how often does he go out with Eric?"

"Eric never goes out without Cain," Alicia said. "Never. My father is deathly afraid that someone will kidnap him."

"Has anyone ever tried?"

"No, but he's read some stories about the children of rich men being kidnapped back East."

"Why doesn't he have a bodyguard for you?"

She looked at him like he was a dull schoolboy.

"I'm a daughter," she said. "Who would want to kidnap a daughter?"

Clint was starting to think that the elder Pemberton did not have a very high opinion of women.

"What about your mother?" he asked. "What does she think of all this wedding business?"

"My mother died years ago," Alicia said, while looking Clint straight in the eye. "Since then my father has had a . . . succession of women friends, each younger than the last. Right now he's seeing a woman who is only two or three years older than I am."

"Does that make you mad?"

Her eyes flashed but she said, "I learned a long time ago it's no use getting mad at my father, Mr. Adams. It simply does no good."

Abruptly, she pushed her chair back, preparing to leave.

"I have to go," she said. "I really don't know what this accomplished. I can't believe I've told you all this."

"I'm easy to talk to," he said.

"Obviously."

He paid the check and they went outside together.

"Is your friend with the wh—with Jennifer now?"

"Yes."

"It's odd, isn't it?" she asked. "A man his age becoming . . . infatuated with a younger woman?"

"Not if your father is any example," he said.

"Touché," she said, turned and walked away.

TWENTY-ONE

"Why do you care if I'm happy?" Jennifer asked Jacob Webster.

"That . . . is very difficult to explain."

"Why don't you try?"

"Do you know who I am?"

"No."

"I am the brothel inspector." He took out the badge the state of Missouri had given him, with "Brothel Inspector" stamped around the number "68."

"So?"

"I was inspecting the premises yesterday."

She looked at him and shrugged.

He walked over to the wall where the moving panel was, removed the chair from in front of it. By poking and prodding he was able to open the panel.

"What's that?"

"You don't know?"

She shook her head.

"It's a panel that's used to rob customers. When they take off their pants the whore usually places them somewhere near the panel so somebody can reach in and pick the pockets."

She looked confused.

"I didn't know that."

"I was in there yesterday," he said. "I found it and was inspecting it when I opened this panel and saw you." He didn't bother saying how the man's pants had been on the chair right near the panel, surely no accident.

"So?"

"I saw your face while the man was . . . while he was on top of you," he said. "You didn't look happy."

She stared at him.

"In your job you meet lots of whores, don't you?"

"Yes."

"How many of them are happy doing what they're doing?"

"Actually," he said, "quite a few."

"Really?"

"Yes," he said. "I have found that many of the women have a choice and would rather do this than work in a store, or a saloon, or be some merchant or cowpoke's husband. Don't you know any of the women here who feel that way?"

"I've only been here two months," she said. "I haven't really made any friends."

"What about the young man you were with?"

"What about him?"

"He says he rich, wants to take you away from all this."

"You want to know about him?" she asked. "His sister was here earlier, also asking questions."

The woman they had followed into the place.

"That means nothing to me," he said. "I am not interested in him or his sister. It's you I'm interested in."

She stared up at him, toyed with the neckline of her nightgown.

"Do you want to go to bed?"

"No!" he snapped. "I'm not interested in you that way."

"Then how?"

"I . . . just want you to be happy."

"Why?" she asked. "I don't understand."

He closed the panel and sat heavily on the wooden chair.

"To tell you the truth, I don't understand, either," he said. "I saw your face through that panel and it . . . was like I was . . . hypnotized. After I left I couldn't stop thinking about your face."

"My face?"

"Yes."

After a moment she asked, "Are you going to tell anyone about the . . . the panel?"

"No."

"You could have Bertha arrested, couldn't you?"

"Arrested, and shut down," he said. "Yes."

"Then why aren't you?"

"Because of you." He looked down at his shoes.

"So if I leave with you, you won't turn her in?"

He looked up at her quickly.

"No! It's not like that. Why are you trying to make this like that?"

"Because," she said, "I don't believe you. I don't believe that you just want me to be happy."

"Why not?"

"Because men aren't like that."

"Maybe," he said, "it's just most of the men you've met who aren't like that."

"Not most," she said, "all."

"That rich young man, he sounded sincere."

"Oh, sure," she said, "he's sincere. He's getting married next month, but first he wants to take me out of here and set me up somewhere so he can sneak away from his wife and be with me whenever he wants. And I would have to stay where he puts me and just wait for him. And he's wondering why I don't jump at the chance? Are you wondering?"

"I was," he said. "Not anymore."

"Look . . . I think you should go," she said. "I'm fine, really. I'll stay here and . . . and . . . I'm fine."

"Jennifer—"

"Just go," she said.

He stood up.

"I'll go, but I won't leave St. Louis. I'm at a hotel called the Drury. If you change your mind send me a message there. Otherwise . . . I'll come back and check on you."

"Don't come back here," she said. "Just don't. I . . . I don't believe you."

"I know," he said, "I know."

He left.

TWENTY-TWO

Clint and Webster met at Clint's hotel, decided not to sit and talk, but to do it while moving. They went outside and just started walking while Webster went first and told Clint about his conversation with Jennifer.

"Sounds like she's been hurt a lot for someone so young," Clint said.

"All the more reason why I want to see that she's happy," Webster told him.

"Jacob, it doesn't seem to me she wants your help."

"She may not want it," he said, "but she needs it."

"It sounds like you may have to convince her of that."

"I will. What did you find out from the other girl. You know, she's the sister of—"

"Eric Pemberton."

"What?"

"Do you know the name Pemberton?"

"Of course. He's one of the richest men in Missouri."

"Well, the young man you saw is his son."

"And the girl you talked to his daughter?"

"Right."

"What do they want with Jennifer?"

"They don't want Jennifer to be with Eric."

"Well, she doesn't want to be," Webster said. "She doesn't care about his money."

"You and I know that," Clint said, "but his father doesn't know it."

"What will he do?'

"He may have already done it."

"What do you mean?"

"He may be the one who sent that man earlier today to scare her."

"That bastard! Do you see? She needs protecting."

"Jacob—"

The older man stopped walking and grabbed Clint's arm.

"That's it."

"What's it?"

"You have to protect her," Webster said, urgently. "You have to be her bodyguard."

"Oh, no, Jacob," Clint said. "I said I'd help you, but that doesn't include bodyguarding a whore in a whorehouse. That would be impossible, given her business."

"I don't want to guard her against customers," Webster said, "just against Pemberton and his men."

Clint was looking for a way out.

"I tell you what I'll do," he said, finally. "I'll go and talk to Pemberton. I'll convince him that there's no need to send anyone after Jennifer ever again, that she has no interest at all in his son."

Webster looked crushed.

"I guess that'll have to do."

"That's as far as I'll go—and that's pretty far."

"Would you guard her if I paid you?"

"Do you have any money?"

"Well . . . no . . ."

"It wouldn't matter if you did," Clint said. "I'm not hiring out as a bodyguard."

"All right," Webster said, "all right. Talk to Pemberton, then. Maybe that will accomplish something."

"After that I'm afraid I'm done," Clint said. "I'll be leaving St. Louis after the weekend."

"I understand," Webster said. "My obsessions are not your concern."

"This doesn't have to be an obsession, Jacob," Clint said. "You can only do so much and if she doesn't want your help, then you'll just have to go on with your life."

"I realize that."

"Good."

"I realize it," Webster said, turning to walk away, "but that doesn't mean I'll be able to do it."

TWENTY-THREE

As prominent a family as the Pembertons were it was not hard for Clint to find out where they lived. When he was standing out in front of their home in the Shaw section of St. Louis, which was near a big park, he wondered what the hell he was doing there. Why would William Pemberton even consider talking to him? What went on in the Pemberton family was none of his business.

Still, the more he thought about it the more he realized that Jennifer did need someone's help. She had definitely been threatened by someone. Alicia Pemberton seemed fairly sure that it had been this bodyguard fella, Cain. So Clint figured he was here to find out if that was true and, if it was, then he had to convince Pemberton that there were no reasons for Cain to ever visit Jennifer again—unless, of course, the man felt the need for a whore.

Well, with that settled in his head he proceeded up the walk to the door of the Pemberton home and knocked. He was surprised when the door was opened by Alicia.

She stared at him in surprise for a moment and then asked, "Did you follow me home?"

"Believe it or not, I didn't," he said.

"How did you get here, then?"

"Your house is not a hard one to find, Alicia," he said. "All I had to do was ask around."

"And what are you doing here?"

"I came to see your father."

That surprised her even more.

"What for?"

"Just to talk."

"About what?"

"What do you think?" Clint asked. "I want to find out if he sent a big bodyguard to bully and threaten a young whore."

"Oh? And then what will you do?"

"I'll try to convince him it was a mistake, one that doesn't have to be repeated."

"Look, Clint," she said, "I know you want to help—"

"I want to help Jennifer," Clint said, "and my friend, Jacob." She shook her head at him.

"A whore and a brothel inspector?" she asked. "These are the people you call your friends?"

"As a matter of fact," Clint said, "yes, they are. Now, is your father in, or shall I come back?"

"He's here," she said, "but I don't know if he'll see you. Come in and I'll ask him."

She backed away to let him enter the large entry foyer. She closed the front door and said, "Wait here."

"What? No butler?"

She turned to look at him, saw that he was kidding, and said, "He has the day off." She pointed her finger at him. "Stay there."

"I'll wait right here."

Alicia disappeared down a hallway.

William Pemberton looked up from his desk as his daughter entered his office.

"What can I do for you, honey?"

"Daddy, there's a man here to see you."

"Tell him I'm busy."

"His name is Clint Adams."

Pemberton looked up from his work. "Adams. I know that name, don't I?"

"Yes."

"Wait, wait . . . he's a very famous man, isn't he?"

"I guess so."

"Sure he is," Pemberton said. He snapped his fingers. "The Gunsmith, right?"

"That's right."

"Well, my God," Pemberton said, forgetting his work. "What does he want here?"

"He . . . wants to talk to you."

"Well, show him in, daughter, show him in," Pemberton said. "We can't keep a prominent man like him waiting on the doorstep, can we?"

Alicia hesitated, wondering if she should tell her father what it was Clint Adams wanted. She decided not to. She decided to wait and see if Clint could handle her father, or if William Pemberton would come out the winner—like always.

"I'll bring him right in."

When Alicia came back down the hall she put her hand out to Clint, as if to hold his.

"Come with me," she said. "My father will see you now."

"Did you tell him why I wanted to see him?" Clint asked, following her down the hall.

She looked back at him over her shoulder and said, "No, I thought you should be the one to do that."

TWENTY-FOUR

"Daddy," Alicia said, entering her father's office, "allow me to introduce Clint Adams."

William Pemberton stood up, remained behind his desk, and stuck his hand out.

"Mr. Adams, it's a pleasure."

Clint had to cross the room to take the man's hand. He wondered if this was simply one of a powerful man's ploys to take control of the situation immediately.

"Clint, my father, William Pemberton."

Clint shook the man's hand and said, "Thank you for seeing me with no appointment. I know how busy you must be."

"Nonsense," Pemberton said, "you're prominent in your own right, Mr. Adams, and you made the time to come and see me. May I offer you a drink? A cigar?"

"No, nothing, thank you."

"Then have a seat and you can tell me what brings you here." Pemberton sat and looked at Alicia. "That'll be all, dear. Thank you."

"Yes, Daddy."

Dismissed, she left the room, but did not go far. She remained out in the hall so she could listen.

• • •

Jacob Webster sat in the café across from the St. Louis Brothel Company. He sat by the window—at the very table where Cain Barrett always sat when Eric Pemberton was inside—and watched the doorway. It was late afternoon and the brothel was open, but he thought perhaps Jennifer might not be working, after her earlier ordeal, and her conversations with Alicia Pemberton and himself. He wondered if she might come outside, giving him a chance to talk to her again. He had to make her see that he truly just wanted to help her.

"So," William Pemberton said, "what brings you to my door, Mr. Adams? How can I help you?"

"This is kind of difficult," Clint said. "Um, I'm involved in something that is probably none of my business, but . . ."

"Well, come out with it, then," Pemberton said, "and we'll see if I can be of any help."

"It's about a girl who works at a brothel your son frequents."

"My son?" Pemberton was immediately on the defensive. "What do you know about my son?"

"Only that he's supposed to be getting married next month, and that he's taken a liking to a young prostitute, which could be a potential problem for you."

Pemberton's eyes narrowed.

"I know your reputation, Adams," he said, dropping the "Mr.", "but I've never heard anything about you being a blackmailer."

"And I'm not one now, Mr. Pemberton," Clint said. "I'm here to tell you that the girl is no danger to you or your son. She has no intention of leaving the brothel to take your son up on his offer."

"How do you know this?"

"I've spoken with her." He decided to leave Jacob Webster out of it, for now.

"And you believe her?"

"Yes."

"That she'd rather toil in a whorehouse than allow my son to take care of her?"

"Yes."

"Why?"

"It's very simple," Clint said. "She doesn't like your son."

William Pemberton glared daggers across his desk at Clint.

"Are you telling me some filthy little whore thinks she's too good for my son?"

"I'm not telling you that at all," Clint said. "I thought you'd be pleased that she wasn't interested."

"I don't want it getting around that some whore rejected my son."

"And it won't."

"Oh no? See here, Adams, what did you come here for?"

"Only to plead the girl's case," Clint said. "She wants to be left alone. She doesn't want to be threatened by your men, anymore."

"My men?"

"Doesn't a man named Cain Barrett work for you?"

"Yes, he does," Pemberton said. "Cain is my son's bodyguard."

"Well, apparently he visited the girl today and scared the wits out of her," Clint said. "Are you saying that he wasn't doing that on your orders?"

"I employ Cain to protect my son, Adams," Pemberton said, "not to go around threatening whores."

"So it wasn't him?"

"It better not have been, or he'll be fired!"

"I see."

"Now, if there's nothing else—"

"Have I convinced you that the girl is no danger to your wedding plans for your son?"

"To tell you the truth, Adams," Pemberton said, "you haven't convinced me of a damned thing . . . and your time is up."

TWENTY-FIVE

Clint walked out the door and almost collided with Alicia, who frantically held her forefinger to her lips and waved at him to follow her back along the hallway.

She took him not only to the entry foyer, but out the door and onto the front porch, which wrapped around the house. She walked him to the side of the house opposite her father's office, as far away from her father's ears as they could get.

"You made him mad," she said.

"I don't understand him," Clint said. "He doesn't want Jennifer to go with Eric, does he?"

"No."

"Then why is he upset?"

"Because you told him that she was rejecting Eric," Alicia explained. "He can't have a whore reject a Pemberton."

"Alicia, what will he do?"

"I'm not sure," she said. "He'll probably offer her money to leave town."

"He doesn't strike me as the type of man to part with his money easily," Clint said.

"No, you're right," she said. "He's not."

"Will he send Cain after her?"

"I don't know," she said. "Cain is Eric's bodyguard. My

father sometimes uses other . . ." She stopped.

"Other men to do his dirty work for him?' Clint finished. "Others to do his killing?"

"My father doesn't kill people!" she snapped.

"Do you really think he got all of this without doing anyone any harm?" he asked, waving his arms.

"Maybe that's the way you get things in the West," she said. "He worked for what he has."

"I'm sure he did."

"I don't think I want to see you or talk to you anymore, Mr. Adams," she said, like a little girl, loyal to her father.

"I understand, Alicia," Clint said.

"Do you?"

"Yes," he said. "He's your father. No matter what happens—no matter who gets hurt—that doesn't change."

"Good-bye, Mr. Adams."

"Good-bye, Alicia," he said, and stepped down from the porch. When he reached the end of the walk he looked back. She was still standing there, hugging herself as if chilled.

And maybe she was.

Webster was about to give up and leave when the front door of the brothel opened and Jennifer stepped out. After being frightened the way she had been that morning—and maybe even threatened—he thought it was a brave thing to do, leave the house on her own.

She came down the steps, turned right and began to walk. Webster hurriedly paid his check, and left the café to follow her.

When Alicia reentered the house her father was coming into the entry foyer from the hallway.

"Is he gone?" he demanded.

"Yes, Daddy, he's gone."

"I don't want him in this house again."

"I told him to go away," she said. "He won't be back."

"Where's your brother?"

"I don't know," she said. "He's out."

"When he comes back tell Cain I want to see him."

She swallowed and asked, "About what?"

"Never mind, little girl," Pemberton said, patting her cheek, "never mind. Just tell him."

Eric and Cain came in about an hour later, while Alicia was sitting in the living room, thinking about everything she had heard that afternoon, everything that Clint Adams had said.

"Hey, Alicia," Eric said, when he saw her. "What are you doing?"

"Just sitting."

"Hello, Alicia," Cain said.

"Hello, Cain," she replied. A shiver ran down her back, as it always did when he first spoke to her. It left her feeling chilled to the bone. "Daddy said he wanted to see you when you came in."

"See me?" Eric asked.

"No," she said, "he wants to see Cain."

"Thanks, Alicia," Cain said. "I'll go and see what he wants."

As Cain left Eric moved closer to his sister and asked, "Why do you treat him so coldly?"

"Because he makes me feel cold," she said.

"He's in love with you, Al—"

"Never mind that," she said, grabbing his arm. "Sit here with me. We have to talk."

TWENTY-SIX

"Close the door," Pemberton told Cain, "and have a seat."

Cain obeyed both commands.

"What's wrong?" he asked.

"I just had a visitor."

"Who?"

"Clint Adams."

"Who's that?"

Pemberton gave his man a disgusted look.

"Are you really that stupid?"

Cain just stared at him.

"Clint Adams? The Gunsmith?"

"Him?" Cain said. "I thought he was dead. Isn't he . . . old?"

"He looked alive when he was in that chair a little while ago."

"Still," Cain said, "he's got to be . . . old."

"Not that old."

"What did he want?"

"He wanted me—and you—to leave that whore alone."

"What? How did he get involved in this?"

"I don't know," Pemberton said, "but I'd like to find out."

"From who?"

"Who else?" Pemberton asked. "That is, if you're not too afraid to go and see her again."

"Afraid of who?" Cain asked. "An old legend? When do you want me to see her."

"Tonight," Pemberton said, "now. I'll keep Eric home. Go and find out how she knows this Gunsmith."

"Why don't I just go and see him?" Cain asked. "Take care of the problem at the source?"

"No," Pemberton said, "I have somebody else in mind for that job."

"Who?"

"Somebody who's more used to that kind of . . . confrontation," Pemberton said.

"I can handle him."

"I can't remember the last time I saw you wearing a gun and holster," Pemberton said.

Cain patted the gun he was wearing under his arm in a shoulder rig and said.

"This is the only holster I ever need."

"Still," Pemberton said, "go and see the girl. I'll take care of the rest."

Cain shrugged and said, "You're the boss."

"Kind of you to remember that. Now get going—and don't bother telling Eric."

"Right."

"Tell him I want to see him."

Cain nodded and stood up.

"What's going on?" Eric asked.

"Eric, there may be some trouble."

"What kind of trouble?"

"Over that girl."

"What girl?"

"Come on, Eric," Alicia said. "The whore, Jennifer."

"How do you know about her?"

"I know, Daddy knows—"

"He does?"

"Yes."

"Who told him?"

"Who do you think?"

Eric looked at her helplessly, then said, "Wait, you don't mean . . . Cain, do you?"

"Well, who else?"

"He wouldn't do that, Alicia."

"And why not?"

"Because he's my friend."

"Eric, wake up!" she said. "Cain works for Daddy."

"But . . . why would he tell?"

"Never mind why," she said. "I think that girl is in trouble if you don't tell Daddy you've given her up."

"Give her up? I can't."

She sat back and stared at her brother.

"My God, Eric," she said, "you're not in love with her, are you?"

"Of course not," he said, "but Alicia, I'm getting married next month, and have you taken a good look at Mary Jane?"

"So this is just about sex?"

"Of course."

"But . . . you can have sex with anybody. You can take a mistress after you're married, the way Daddy had always done."

"That's what I'm doing!"

"Eric . . . she's a whore."

"Not after I take her out of that place."

"Eric—"

She stopped when Cain reappeared in the doorway of the living room.

"Your father wants to see you, Eric."

"What about?"

"He doesn't confide in me," the man said. "I'm going out."

"Where?" Eric asked.

"I don't confide in you, Eric," Cain said, and left.

"Where's he going?" Eric asked, aloud.

"I think I can guess," Alicia said.

"Alicia—"

"You'd better go and see what Daddy wants," she said, getting up from the sofa.

"But if he's going where you think—"

"Eric," she said, "go and see Daddy. I'll take care of the rest."

"How?"

"I think I know somebody who can help," she said. "Now go, before he comes looking for you and we're both stuck here."

Eric stood up and walked uncertainly from the room, then down the hall. Alicia went to the front door, opened it, peered out to make sure Cain was gone, and then left.

"Jennifer."

She turned, her eyes wide with fright, then saw that it was Webster.

"What do you want?"

"Just to walk with you a while," he said. "Is that all right?"

She seemed to think about it.

"You shouldn't be out alone," he said.

She thought some more, then said, "All right, but we just walk. No talking."

"All right," Webster agreed, "no talking."

TWENTY-SEVEN

Alicia hitched a horse to a buggy and drove herself to Clint's hotel as quickly as she could, hoping he had gone back there from the Pemberton house and not somewhere else. She stopped the buggy in front of the hotel and ignored the doorman as he started to say, "Ma'am, you can't leave—" She ran past him, saying, "I won't be long."

He watched her run inside and, had he not recognized her as a member of the affluent Pemberton family, probably would have had the buggy moved.

Alicia ran up to the front desk and asked the clerk if he knew where Clint Adams was.

Clint, upon returning from the Pemberton house and finding that Webster was not waiting for him at the hotel, decided to go into the bar and while away the time with a beer or two while he waited to see if the man would return.

However, instead of Jacob Webster finally appearing in the doorway of the bar—he had left word with the desk this was where he would be—-it was Alicia Pemberton who showed up. She saw him and ran over to his table.

"If you've come to apologize for kicking me out—"

"Shut up!" she said. "I think your friend is in trouble."

"What friend?"

"The girl, the whore, what's her name?" Alicia said.

"Jennifer?"

"Yes."

"What kind of trouble?"

"I'll tell you on the way," she said. "I have a buggy outside."

"On the way where?"

"Where do you find a whore?" she said, impatiently. "Come on, I think Cain is on his way over there right now."

"After the talk I had with your father?"

"*Because* of the talk you had with my father!"

Suddenly, that made sense to Clint. Why hadn't he seen it before? Pemberton was going to want to know what Clint's stake was in all this. Who better to ask than the girl herself.

"Are you coming?"

"I'm coming," he said, and ran out of the bar after her.

When Cain reached the whorehouse he mounted the front steps and tried the door. It was open for business, so the knob turned and the door opened. He stepped inside and was immediately confronted by the big madam, Bertha.

"Welcome to—you! What do you want here?"

"Same thing I wanted last time, Ma'am," Cain said. "To talk to Jennifer. Is she in her room?"

"No, she's not working tonight because you scared her."

"I'll check for myself, if you don't mind," he said, starting for the stairs.

"I do mind," she said, getting in front of him.

"Now, Ma'am, you don't want to do that."

"You get out of here!" she snapped.

"Get out of my way, old woman," Cain said, impatiently. He put both hands on Bertha to move her, but she wouldn't budge. He decided to put his legs into it, braced himself, and pushed her aside.

"Bubba!" she shouted.

Cain started up the stairs but from the top Bubba, the big black man, was coming down.

"Show this man out, Bubba," Bertha said.

Bubba smiled and said, "With pleasure, Miz Bertha."

TWENTY-EIGHT

When Alicia and Clint pulled up in front of the St. Louis Brothel Company the front door was missing and there was a man lying on his back at the base of the steps. On the steps were Bertha and some of the whores who worked there. Two of the girls were leaning over the fallen man, and one of them—a bosomy blonde—had his head in her lap.

"What happened?" Clint asked, stepping down from the buggy.

"That crazy man came back, that's what happened," Bertha said. "I told Bubba to throw him out, but he threw poor Bubba right through the door and out into the street."

At that moment, as if on cue, poor Bubba moaned. Clint looked down at him and he could have sworn the black man winked at him. He might have gotten thrown through a door and down a flight of steps, but he didn't seem to be in too much pain at the moment.

"Did he get Jennifer?"

"She wasn't here," Bertha said.

"Where is she?"

"I gave her the night off," Bertha said, "and she went out."

"Alone?"

"What was I supposed to do?" Bertha demanded. "Be her goddamned chaperone?"

"Did you see which way she went when she left?"

"No," Bertha said, but one of the other girls said, "I was looking out the window when she left and she went that way." She pointed to the left. "Then I saw a man follow her."

"A man? What man?" Clint asked.

"I don't know.'

"Describe him."

"He was older, in his fifties, with white hair, real nice clothes," the girl said. "That's all I know."

It was enough. Jacob Webster had followed Jennifer down the street.

"All right," Clint said, "we'll go looking for them."

"What do we do, in the meantime?" Bertha asked.

"Well, get yourself a new door," he said, "and don't move him until he's ready."

The black man looked up at Clint, but then his view was blocked when two big breasts came down on his face as the girl whose lap he was resting in said, "It's okay, Bubba, you'll be okay."

As he climbed back up onto the buggy next to Alicia, Clint had the feeling Bubba was already pretty okay.

"You keep your word, don't you?" Jennifer asked.

"Pardon me?" Jacob Webster asked.

"I asked you not to talk. We been walkin' an hour and you ain't said a word."

"That's what you wanted."

"I don't understand you, Mister."

"Jacob."

"Jacob," she said. "You don't even know me, but you say you want to help me."

"That's right."

"Why?"

"That's a very good question," Webster said. "I've been

wondering that myself ever since I first saw you, but I can't come up with a good explanation."

"What *can* you come up with?" she asked.

"All I know is that when I first saw your face," he said, "I knew you needed my help."

"And the first time you saw my face," she said, "Eric Pemberton was pounding away at me."

"Yes."

She shook her head.

"You're a strange man, Jacob."

"I know."

TWENTY-NINE

"Where do we look?" Alicia asked, as they drove away from the scene in front of the whorehouse.

"I don't know," Clint said. "I guess we'll just have to drive around. Hopefully, they'll stay on foot and we'll find them before Cain does."

"And then what?"

"I'll have to warn the girl that I may have made things worse for her by going to your father."

"You were trying to help."

"She may have been better off," he said, "if I had kept my nose out of her business."

"And what about your friend?"

"I should let him worry about his own problems, too."

"Don't be so hard on yourself for trying to be helpful," she said.

"Helpful is one thing," Clint said. "How do I know I wouldn't have gotten that girl killed if she'd been there when Cain got there?"

"I still can't believe my father would tell Cain to kill her."

"What then? Frighten her? He did that earlier today. Besides, your father wouldn't be there, would he? What if it went bad? What if she spit in his face? What would his reaction be?"

"He's . . . not an animal," Alicia said, lamely.

"He's not? Or you're not sure?"

"I'm . . . you're right, I'm not sure. He . . . frightens me. Look what he did to that big black man. Cain is not very big, but he's . . . scary."

"And what else?"

"What?"

"There's something else you're not saying."

"Well . . . Eric seems to think Cain . . . wants me."

"And how do you feel about that?"

"It makes me cold. Just the thought of a man like him putting his hands on me . . ." She shivered.

"How does your father feel about it?'

"I don't know if he knows."

"I'll wager if your brother knows, your father knows, too. Has Cain ever said anything?"

"No."

"Probably because your father won't let him," Clint said. "I doubt he'd want his daughter getting involved with the hired help."

"You're probably right." She looked him in the eye. "You seem to know him pretty well after one meeting."

"Not him, exactly," Clint said, "but men like him. Men a lot like him."

Webster and Jennifer were walking aimlessly, not knowing where they were going. At one point they started to talk, to chat, like old friends. Webster told her about growing up in England and coming to America to make his fortune in the "American West."

"This was as far as I got," he said. "I have never been further west of the Mississippi than this."

"Neither have I," she said. "I came here from Boston."

"How did you end up in the . . . house?"

"I was recommended," she said. "I came with a letter of

introduction from a friend in Boston who said I should come here if I got desperate. Obviously . . . I did."

"But . . . how long did you intend to stay?"

"Until I saved some money."

"And have you?"

"Some," she said. "Not a lot. Most of the money goes to Bertha, and to whoever owns the house."

"Bertha doesn't own it?"

She put her hand to her mouth.

"I forgot I'm talking to the brothel inspector."

"Don't worry," he said. "If I'm not going to say anything about the panel rooms, I won't say anything about this, either."

"Well . . . she's supposed to be the owner, everyone thinks she is, but there's someone else."

"Do you know who it is?"

"No, I don't."

He touched her arm to stop her and turned to face her.

"Jennifer, I'm just an old man—"

"Not so terribly old," she said.

"Old enough to know better," he said. "I truly am not interested in you the same way young Eric is. If you would like to leave the brothel, and St. Louis, I can help you."

"How?"

"We can go together," he said. "We can be travelling companions. Together we can discover the west."

"People would talk," she said. "A young woman and . . ."

"An old man," he finished for her.

"I was going to say 'older' man," she said, with a smile.

"We can travel as daughter and father, or grandfather, or as niece and uncle. I don't care. It's time for me to make a change in my life. Don't you feel the same way?"

"Well . . . yes," she said, "I have been feeling a . . . a longing to move on with my life."

"Then we can do it together."

"What about Bertha? I was supposed to stay six months, at least."

"Did you sign a contract?"

"No."

"Then she can't hold you to anything, can she?"

"N-no, but—"

"Do you feel any loyalty to her?"

"Not really," she said. "After all, she does take most of my money."

He took hold of her shoulders.

"I think this was destiny, Jennifer," he said. "That we should meet at a time when we both want to move on. What do you say?"

"I—I don't know, Jacob," she said. "I—I'll have to think about it."

"That's no problem," he said. "No problem at all. That's all I ask, in fact, is that you think it over."

"I'd better get back now," she said. "It'll be getting dark soon."

"I'll walk you back."

"All right."

They started back.

"When are you supposed to give your answer to Eric Pemberton?" he asked. "Monday, is it?"

"Yes."

"Did you have any intention at all—"

"No," she said. "None at all. I—I don't like people with money, Jacob. They think they can buy anything they want. He can buy me for an hour, but he can't buy *me*!" She looked at him with pleading eyes. "Does that make sense?"

"It makes all the sense in the world."

THIRTY

William Pemberton rarely went into his Market Street office but today was special. There were certain contacts he could only make through the office, and Benny Doran was one of them. Pemberton had one of his young men—interns, he called them, working for him to learn about the business world—go across the Eads bridge to East St. Louis, Illinois, to find Benny. Pemberton told the young man to look in the worst saloons and bars he could find. The young man was thinking that those were the *only* kinds of saloons one would find in East St. Louis—a place where no law abiding St. Louis citizen would be caught, er, dead.

The young man's name was Walter Carter, and he was extremely nervous as he walked from saloon to saloon looking for Benny Doran. There were several times when young Carter didn't think he was going to get out with his wallet—or his life—but he knew that if he wanted to get anywhere working for William Pemberton he had to succeed at this little errand.

However, in a saloon called the Broken Bottle he thought he had come to the end of his luck.

"Doran, you say?" the grizzled bartender repeated. He looked down the bar. "Hey, boys, this young feller is looking for Benny Doran."

"He is?" Carter looked to see who had spoken and saw a big, full-bearded man with small, piggy eyes coming toward him, followed by two others of the same ilk. The stench of the three men reached him before they did.

"Maybe we'll do," the spokesman said.

"He's a pretty one," one of them said.

"Real pretty clothes," another said.

The spokesman with the piggy eyes looked Carter up and down and said, "And real pretty—" but he was cut off.

"That's enough, boy!" a big voice boomed out.

All three men froze at the sound of the voice, as did Carter. He turned and saw a big man, bigger than the man with the piggy eyes, not as hairy, but no less frightening to look at.

"Hi, Benny," Piggy-eyes said.

"Were you boys thinking' about botherin' my friend, here?" Benny Doran asked.

"No, Benny," Piggy-eyes said, "we wasn't botherin' him—was we, Mister? We wuz just gonna help him find you."

"Help him find me?' Doran asked. "You don't even know who he is, why would you help him find me?"

"Well, you said he wuz your friend—" Piggy-eyes started.

"Ah, just go back to your beers," Doran said to the three of them. "You ain't worth my time. Hey, sonny!"

"Y-yes?' Carter said, assuming the big man was talking to him.

"Get me a beer and bring it to that table in the back."

"Y-yessir."

"And bring one for yourself."

"I don't drink—"

"I don't talk to nobody who don't drink with me."

"Y-yessir."

Doran walked to the table and sat down, waiting patiently for Carter to bring him his beer.

Walter Carter got the two beers and hurried across the

saloon with them, managing to spill not a drop even though his hands were shaking.

"Siddown!" Doran told him.

He did.

Doran leaned forward. "Was you just gonna let them have you?"

"H-have me?"

"You got speak up for yourself, boy," Doran said. "They wuz gonna make boy-ass of you."

"B-boy-ass?" Carter didn't know what that was, and had the feeling he didn't want to know.

Doran sat back.

"Never mind," he said. "You been hittin' saloons up and down the street sayin' you're lookin' for me. Why?"

"M-Mr. Pemberton sent me to find you."

"Pemberton?" Doran said. "He's got Cain Barrett workin' for him now, don't he?"

"Y-yes, I believe he does."

"So what's he want with me?"

"H-he didn't tell me that, sir," Carter said. "He just told me to tell you he wants to meet with you?"

"And where does he want this meeting to take place?' Doran asked. "Am I supposed to march up to his office without the proper wardrobe? Huh?"

"No, sir," Carter said. "He said that you would know where to meet him."

"The man wants to use me for the first time in two years and he thinks I know where to meet him?"

"Well, I hope you do, sir," Carter said, "I mean, I certainly don't know anything about—"

"I know where to meet him," Doran said. "Don't worry about it. Just go and tell him midnight tonight."

"M-midnight?"

"That's right."

"W-where?"

"He *knows* where, don't he?"

"Of course," Carter said. "Sorry."

"Now get your ass out of here before I start thinkin' it's pretty, myself," Doran said. "Git!"

"Yes, sir!" Carter said and, not having to be told twice, stood up and got!

THIRTY-ONE

"Well," Alicia said, as it started to get dark, "if we can't find them maybe Cain can't, either."

"That's a good point," Clint said. "Let's just go back to the brothel. If they're not there we can give up and get something to eat."

"That sounds like a good idea to me," Alicia said. "I'm famished."

Webster walked Jennifer back to the brothel and they both stopped at the base of the steps. There were pieces of wooden door strewn about, and the door that was now in place was obviously a new one.

"I wonder what happened here?" Jennifer asked.

"You can find out when you go inside."

"You're not coming in?"

He shook his head.

"I don't think we should be seen together," he said, "just in case you decide to take me up on my offer."

"I'll let you know, Jacob, I really will," she said.

"That's fine," he said. "I'll be waiting."

She went up the steps and into the house. He turned and started to walk away, wondering if he would get his answer before Eric Pemberton got his.

He was walking past an alley when someone grabbed him and pulled him into it.

Alicia drove the buggy right up to the front of the brothel and stopped. They saw the same thing Webster and Jennifer had seen—pieces of wood, a new door—only they knew what had happened.

"They got it fixed real quick," she said.

"I'll just go up and see if she came back."

"All right."

Clint got down from the buggy and walked up the steps. He knocked and the door was answered by Bertha.

"Did she come back?"

"Just a few minutes ago."

"Did she say where she'd been?"

"Just out walking."

"And she didn't run into anyone?"

"She didn't say," Bertha said.

"Well, as long as she's safe," he said.

"That's what I was thinking, too."

"All right," Clint said. "I'll be going, then."

"Will you do what you can to keep that crazy man from coming back here?" she asked.

"Yes, I will."

"Thank you," she said, and closed the door.

Clint walked back to the buggy and was about to climb aboard when Alicia asked, "What's that?"

"What?"

He looked down the street where she was pointing. It was getting dark but he saw a man stagger from an alley, drunkenly.

"Looks like a man drunk," she said.

"Or injured," he said, as he saw that the man had white hair. He immediately started running and caught up to Jacob Webster just as he started to fall. Clint caught him, lowering him to the ground. He'd been thoroughly beaten up, his face a mass of bumps and blood. He was holding his sides, too, as if they hurt, as well.

Clint heard the buggy pull up to them and Alicia asked, "Who is it?"

"It's Webster," Clint said. "We've got to get him to a hospital."

He picked the man up and carried him to the buggy. They couldn't all fit so he said to Alicia, "Take him. I'll come as fast as I can."

"All right," she said. "I'll take him to St. John's. Any driver will know where it is."

"Okay," he said, "go!"

Clint wondered if the man would still be alive by the time he got there.

When he reached St. John's he found Alicia sitting out in the lobby.

"Where is he?"

"They're looking at him now," she said. "He started to cough up blood on the way here."

"Did he say anything?" Clint asked. "Like who did it?"

"No," she said, "but I think we both have a good idea."

"But why?" Clint asked. "Cain was after Jennifer. Why beat Webster up that way?"

"Maybe he was just mad," she said, "and taking it out on him."

"Sonofabitch!" He could feel the rage welling up inside of him.

He started away but she grabbed him with both arms.

"No! Don't go after him in this frame of mind."

"Let go, Alicia."

"At least stay and make sure he's all right," she said, "so when you get your vengeance you'll know what it's for."

He looked at her for a moment, felt the rage subside a bit, and said, "All right, we'll wait."

THIRTY-TWO

William Pemberton glared across his desk at Cain Barrett, who suffered the scrutiny with apparent ease.

"You did what?"

"Taught him a lesson."

"Beat him up?"

"Yes, sir."

"And left him for dead?"

"No, sir," Cain said. "I imagine by now he's in a hospital."

"Why didn't you kill him?"

"I had no orders to."

"And the girl?"

"She wasn't there when I got there," the bodyguard said, "and then there was a scene."

"What kind of scene?"

"Well, the woman who runs the whorehouse—"

"Bertha."

"That's right," Cain said. "She's a big woman—"

"Which is why they call her Big Bertha."

Cain hesitated, then said, "Right. Anyway, she told this big nigger to kick me out—"

"That would be Bubba."

"Yeah," Cain said, "I think she called him that. Anyway,

121

I had to put him through the front door. After that I figured the police might come so I went and hid in the alley, waiting for the girl and the brothel inspector to get back."

"And what happened?"

"They must have come from the other direction, because they didn't pass me."

"And she got back into the house."

"Right."

"So you decided to teach him a lesson."

"Right," Cain said, "which is what I sa—"

"You should have killed him."

"What?"

"I want the brothel inspector," Pemberton said, "the Gunsmith, and the girl dead. Is that clear enough for you?"

"All three?"

"That's right."

"I'd probably need some help with—"

"I'm getting you help.'

"You are?"

Pemberton nodded.

"Who?" Cain asked.

"You'll find out soon," Pemberton said. "We're going to be meeting him at midnight, so don't go anywhere for the next few hours."

"Who is this man?"

"Somebody you don't know," Pemberton said. "But you will."

When the doctor came out Clint and Alicia both approached him. The physician only knew her, since she had brought Webster in, and because she was a Pemberton.

"Miss Pemberton," he said.

"Doctor, this is Clint Adams. He's a friend of Mr. Webster's."

"Mr. Adams," the doctor said, and the two men shook hands.

"How is he, Doctor?"

"Well," the man said, "I'm afraid he's got some cracked ribs, a lot of bruises, a bump on the head, a swollen cheek which may or may not be broken . . . he was pretty well beaten up by somebody who knew what they were doing."

"Are any of the injuries serious?" Clint asked.

"Not really," the doctor said, "although, on a man his age they could be. He won't be going anywhere for a while. He'll have to stay here a few days, at least until all the swellings go down and I can examine him again."

"Can we see him?" Alicia asked.

"I'm afraid not."

"Just for a few minutes," Clint said. "I have an idea who did this, but I need him to—"

"He's unconscious," the doctor said. "He will be for some time, I'm afraid. No, you cannot see him tonight."

"All right, Doctor," Clint said. "Thanks. I'll be taking care of the medical bills—"

"Miss Pemberton has already seen to that," the doctor said. "Also, I'm afraid I'll be notifying the police. Does either of you have a problem with that?"

"No," Alicia said.

"None," Clint said, which he thought allayed any suspicions the doctor might have had that he had done this to Webster.

"All right, then," the doctor said. "I'll probably see the two of you tomorrow."

As the doctor walked away Clint turned and started walking.

"Where are you going?" Alicia asked.

"To see Cain."

"And if you can't find him?"

"Then I'll start with your father."

"Clint, be careful . . ."

"I will be," he said. "You wait here and talk to the police. And Alicia . . . thanks for your help."

"Just be careful," she said, again.

"I will."

THIRTY-THREE

The Shaw Cemetery was where the rich people were buried. Pemberton thought he knew why Benny Doran would pick this place. He'd find it more than a little bit ironic.

Cain looked around uneasily and said, "I hate cemeteries."

Pemberton looked at Cain. He'd never seen the man unnerved, not once in all the time he'd employed him.

"They're just a bunch of dead people, Cain," he said. "Get a grip on yourself."

"Me," a voice said, "I love cemeteries."

Benny Doran stepped from the shadows into the light of the full moon.

"Especially the ones where the rich are buried," he said. "Here, they can't look down their noses at me. Hello, Mr. Pemberton. I understand from that pretty boy you sent to find me you got a job for me?"

"I do, Benny."

"It's been a while since you've needed my services."

"Yes, it has."

"This must be Cain."

"That's right," Cain said. "Who are you?"

"I'm Benny, Cain," Doran said. "How do you do?"

"A lot better once I'm out of this cemetery."

"We can fix that," Benny said, looking at Pemberton. "All we have to do is get Mr. Pemberton to tell me what he wants me to do."

"I want you to work with Cain," Pemberton said. "I want three people dead."

"Dead, like in an accident?" Doran asked.

"Just dead," Pemberton said. "I don't care how it's done."

Benny looked at Cain.

"That all right with you, Cain?"

"First I'm hearing about it," Cain said. "I usually work alone, or with someone I know."

"Me, too," Doran said. He looked at Pemberton again. "The price is gonna have to be right for me and Cain to work together, Mr. Pemberton."

"I'll pay you twice the usual fee."

"And Cain?"

"He's on salary."

"I don't care," Doran said. "If I'm working with a man I want him to have as much to lose or gain as I do."

"All right," Pemberton said. "Cain gets a bonus."

"That all right with you, Mr. Barrett?" Doran asked.

"That's fine with me, Mr. Doran."

Pemberton looked back and forth between the two men and said, "Oh, I can tell you two are going to get along just fine."

Clint banged on the front door of the Pemberton house until it was opened by a young man who bore an uncanny resemblence to William Pemberton.

"You'd be Eric."

"That's right," Eric said. "Who are you?"

"Clint Adams."

Eric took an involuntary step back. He wondered where Cain was.

"What do you want?"

"I want to see Cain," Clint said, "Failing that, I'll settle for your father."

"They're not here."

"You're here alone?"

"That's right."

"Where'd they go?"

"I don't know."

Clint doubted that they had gone to do some harm to Jennifer. Pemberton would send Cain for that, but he wouldn't bother to go along.

"Eric, Jennifer is in danger."

"From who?"

"From your father, and from Cain."

"That's nonsense."

"It's not. Your father was worried about you taking her as a mistress. He thought it would ruin your upcoming marriage."

"I've already talked to my sister about this," Eric said. "I've decided to tell Jennifer I'm taking back my offer."

"That's big of you, since she had no intention of accepting it."

"Well . . . that's fine, then," Eric said. "We'll both get what we want."

"You might get what you want," Clint said. "All she's going to get is dead."

"Why?"

"Because your father is not going to want word to get around that his son was rejected by a whore."

Eric started to speak, then stopped as a strange look came over his face. Suddenly, he was very much his father's son.

"So?"

"What do you mean, so? Why should she die because you wanted to keep her and she said no?"

"She should have thought of that."

"So you're willing to let your father kill her?"

"My father usually knows what's best."

Clint grabbed the front of the boy's shirt and pulled him out the door.

"You little pissant!"

"Hey, let go!" Eric said. "If Cain was here you wouldn't do this. Cain? Cain?"

Eric's cowardice was so palpable Clint thought he could smell it.

"Your friend Cain beat up a friend of mine and put him in the hospital today," Clint said, putting his face right in Eric's.

"What's that got to do with me?"

"You're going to give him a message for me."

"W-what message?"

"He's to stay away from Jacob Webster, and from Jennifer. And, for his own good, tell him to stay away from me."

"Cain won't be afraid of you," Eric said. "He'll come and get you."

"That's what I'm counting on."

"You'll be sorry," Eric said. "When Cain and my father get finished with you, you'll be real sorry."

"You're the sorry one, Eric. I should do to you what Cain did to my friend and leave you here to bleed."

"Hey, hey, wait—"

"Don't worry," Clint said, releasing the younger man. "I'm not—but I'm not going to tell you why." It was because Alicia would never have forgiven him. She loved her brother.

Eric quickly backed into the house and slammed the door in Clint's face.

"Just make sure you give Cain my message," Clint yelled through the door. "Don't give me a reason to come back here, Eric!"

There was no answer, but he thought he could feel Eric's presence on the other side of the door. He banged his fist on the door once, just to startle the young man, then turned and stalked off. It was lucky for Eric that the trip over here had been long enough for some of Clint's anger to drain away.

Still, if Cain had been home, it would have been a different story.

THIRTY-FOUR

Clint went back to the hospital to find that Alicia was gone. The doctor wasn't there but a nurse told him that Jacob Webster was resting comfortably and would most likely sleep through the night.

He went back to his hotel, wondering what William Pemberton had been doing out after midnight, with Cain—his son's bodyguard—leaving Eric home alone. What happened to that fear of kidnapping?

He walked through the empty lobby of his hotel and up to his room. He entered, sniffing the air for perfume and finding none. Apparently Carla Moran had chosen not to come over tonight. That was all right with him. He wasn't sure he could have given her the attention she deserved. Especially when he was thinking of another woman—Alicia Pemberton.

He wondered how Alicia could love her father and her brother, and yet be so different from them?

He had just removed his boots and his trousers when there was a gentle knock on the door. He walked to the door, gun in hand, and asked, "Who is it?"

"It's Alicia."

He had qualms about opening the door to her. It never occurred to him that there might be danger on the other

131

side of the door. Alicia seemed very genuine to him.

He unlocked the door and opened it. She looked him up and down with an amused expression on her face and he realized he was standing there in his underwear, holding a gun.

"Is anything wrong?" he asked, groping behind him for his pants.

"No," she said, "I was just waiting for you to get back. I wanted to hear what happened."

He found his trousers and hastily pulled them on. As he did so she stepped into the room and closed the door behind her.

"You could have gone home and found that out," he said.

"I wanted to find out from you."

He buttoned his pants, then replaced the gun in the holster hanging on the bedpost. Comfortably attired he turned to face her. She was looking at him in a way she had not looked at him since he'd met her.

"Alicia—"

"What happened?" she asked, softly. "Did you see Cain? Or my father?"

"I saw Eric."

"He was home alone?"

"Yes."

"That must mean that Daddy had Cain with him."

"That's what I figured."

"Did Eric tell you where they were?"

"No."

"Did you go in?"

"No. We talked, uh, on the doorstep."

The look on her face changed, became one of concern for her brother.

"You didn't hurt him, did you?"

"No, I didn't. I told him that Jennifer might be in danger from your father, and Cain."

"And what did he say?"

"He said, 'so?' "

"That's all?"

"He said your father usually knew what was best."

"Well, he *does* think that."

"Even when it might mean a girl's life?"

"Clint—"

"He didn't care, Alicia," Clint said. "He didn't care that your father might have Cain kill her."

"We still don't know that."

She walked to the window, but did not move the curtain to look out.

"Look what happened to Jacob. First Cain scared Jennifer, then came back and threw Bubba through a door, and now he's put Jacob in the hospital. Things are escalating, Alicia. What's next?"

She turned to face him, but couldn't look at him. Instead, she stood with her arms folded, looking down at the floor.

"I don't know," she said. "I honestly don't know, Clint."

"Neither do I," he said, "but I know what the logical next step would be for a man like your father."

She looked at him this time.

"What?"

"He doesn't want anyone to know that a whore turned down his son," Clint said. "He'll have her killed, Alicia, and probably Jacob, as well."

She didn't say anything.

"He might even send someone after me."

"Why you?"

"I'm the one who brought him the news," he said, "that a whore rejected his son. Tell me your father is not a prideful man."

"He is," she said, her voice almost a whisper. "He's very prideful."

"Pride makes men do stupid things."

"I know."

"Alicia," he said, "I think you better go home. You don't want to be around me."

Now she looked him directly in the eyes and said, "But I do, Clint. I want to be around you . . . very much."

THIRTY-FIVE

He undressed her slowly, as if afraid he would frighten her away if he went too fast. Having no idea of her experience he wanted to take the time to learn, at leisure, how much she knew or didn't know about being with a man.

She was slender, with pale skin, small breasts, brown nipples with wide aureole. Her legs were long, her thighs strong. He felt their strength as he eased himself between them and she brought them up on either side of him. He kissed her mouth, her neck, her shoulders, her breasts and nipples. She was very sensitive and when his mouth touched her nipples she gasped and tightened her thighs around him. She touched his back lightly with her nails, slid her hands down to brush his thighs, then between them to stroke his swollen penis. Her hands were knowing, so he knew she'd done this before. He stopped treating her like a virgin, rubbed his rigid cock over her coarse bush, her wet slit, finally poked at the entrance with the spongy head and pushed in.

She gasped, uttered one single, sibilant "Yessssss" and began to move with him as he slid in and out of her wetly. He moved his hands down to cup her buttocks, which were slender and smooth. Her body—at twenty-two or -three, he guessed—still had some maturing to do, but her skin felt

like silk, and she smelled sweet and sharp at the same
time—sweet perfume, sharp but not unpleasant perspira-
tion, and the heady odor of her wetness as he drove into
her until, finally, he was ready to explode, and did . . .

"You thought I was a virgin?"

"I thought you might be."

"No," she said. "I've been with two men—one only
once, and the other for . . . a time. Was I too inexperi-
enced?"

"You were wonderful," he said.

"You're the only one who was ever concerned with my
pleasure," she said. "It was . . . a revelation. I didn't know
it could be like this between a man and a woman."

"It's a beautiful thing, Alicia," he said. "It shouldn't be
any other way."

"My brother . . ." she said, as she lay on her back,
". . . he wanted Jennifer because he didn't think he could
get something like this from his future wife."

"Why marry her, then?"

"Because my father arranged it."

"And how does the girl feel about it?"

"Mary Jane?" Alicia said. "She's ecstatic. She's plain
looking, with no prospects except the boys who want her
for her father's money."

"And your brother and father don't want her father's
money?"

"Of course they do, but my family also brings *my* father's
money into the mix."

"I see."

"So if my father wants to kill . . . your friends, it's for
much more of a reason than the fact that a whore turned
my brother down. He's trying to protect this . . . merger. It
will secure a future for Eric."

"What kind of future?"

"Political, I think," she said. "It's my belief that my father wants to take Eric to the governor's mansion—and maybe the White House."

"You're father is a very ambitious man."

"He feels a career in politics has passed him by," she said. "He wants to use all of his resources to make sure it doesn't pass Eric by."

"Does Eric seem like a future politician to you?"

"With my father's guidance," she said, "Eric could be anything."

"Alicia," he said, "you don't believe in murder as a means to an end, do you?"

"No."

"Can you maintain that belief without feeling disloyal to your family if that's the way they choose to go?"

She thought for a moment, then rolled over and pressed herself against him and said, "No."

THIRTY-SIX

Alicia stayed until morning, when they woke together and made love again. This time she was much more enthusiastic, attacking him with an avid mouth, sucking him until he was seconds from exploding and then climbing on top of him to take him inside and finish him . . .

"I want to get to the hospital and see if Jacob's condition has improved," he said, while they dressed.

"That's fine with me," Alicia said. "Breakfast can wait."

"That's my girl," Clint said. "Come on."

Outside, standing across the street, were Benny Doran and Cain Barrett. They were waiting for Clint to come out.

"Adams has to be the first one," Benny said, the night before. "He's the most dangerous."

William Pemberton had left them alone to "get acquainted," and had gone home to find his son Eric almost hysterical. When Pemberton found out that Clint had been to his house he found the two men again and told them that things had to be resolved as soon as possible.

That was when Benny said that Clint had to be first, and Cain agreed. Hence, they were waiting across the street from his hotel for him to come out.

However, when he came out with Alicia, Cain put his arm out to stop Benny from following.

"What is it?' the big man asked.

"The girl."

"So he's got a girl with him," Benny said. "I'll share her with you after he's dead."

"I don't think so."

"Fine," Benny said, "then you can have her. I don't care about the girl."

"I do," Cain said. "That's Alicia, Pemberton's daughter."

"His daughter?" Benny said. "What the hell is she doing with him, then?"

"That's what I'm going to find out. Let's just follow them and see where they go."

"All right," Benny said, "but I'm ready to take him out any time."

"I'll keep that in mind."

Already in their young partnership Cain seemed to have stepped to the forefront as leader. It was a position Benny was not fighting to hold, and one that Cain seemed to want. In truth, Benny was impressed with Cain's poise, despite his youth—his attitude in the graveyard the night before notwithstanding. Benny was a good dozen or so years older, but was secure enough in himself not to have to necessarily be the leader in this pairing.

Then again, he felt sure he could take control any time he wanted, just as easily as he had given it up.

They stepped from their doorway and began to follow Clint and Alicia.

"Where's your sister?" William Pemberton demanded.

"I don't know," Eric said. He continued to eat his breakfast.

"She didn't come home last night."

"She's a big girl," Eric said. "She can take care of herself. Where's Cain?"

The elder Pemberton sat down at the head of the table.

His breakfast was brought in and laid before him.

"He's doing a job for me."

"I wanted to go out today."

"No," Pemberton said. "You'll have to stay in until Cain has finished the job he's on."

"And what job is that?"

"Don't worry about it."

"Was Adams right last night?" Eric asked.

"About what?"

"He said you wanted to kill Jennifer."

"Who?"

"The whore."

"Oh, her."

"And some other friend of his."

"Hmm."

"And maybe even him."

"Well," Pemberton said, "given his reputation lots of people want to kill him."

"Dad—"

"Let it go, Eric," Pemberton said, looking directly at his son. They locked eyes for about five seconds, which was usually all that Eric could take. "Whatever I do, I do it for you, for your future."

"I know that."

"Good," Pemberton said, "then don't question me, boy. Finish your breakfast, find something to do inside for today, and maybe tomorrow. After that . . . well, we'll see."

"All right, Dad."

"There's a good son," Pemberton said. "Now, what the hell has happened to your sister?"

When they reached the hospital they found the doctor with no trouble.

"We're still waiting for the swelling to go down," he said. "It'll take some time."

"But how is he?" Clint asked.

"He's resting easily, right now. That's all I can say."

The doctor walked away. Clint turned to face Alicia.

"What are you going to do today?" he asked.

"Go home, I guess," she said. "I'll have some questions to answer, but maybe I can find out something."

"Like what?"

"Like what my father actually plans to do. What are you going to do?"

"I'll go and talk to Jennifer, tell her about Jacob," he said. "Maybe find out what they talked about yesterday."

"Where can we meet later?"

"At my hotel," he said. "For dinner, say at six."

"All right," she said. "Maybe one of us will know something by then."

"Be careful, Alicia."

She gave him a look that said he was crazy.

"My father would never hurt me, Clint."

He wasn't so sure of that, not after what she'd told him about the way Pemberton treated her, and Eric. He wasn't so sure that the old man wouldn't sacrifice the daughter for the good of the son.

He hoped he was wrong.

THIRTY-SEVEN

"I think we should check with Mr. Pemberton first," Cain said.

"But why?' Benny asked. "They've split up, haven't they?"

"She and Adams have been seen together," Cain said. "Mr. Pemberton may want to change his plans."

"I tell you what," Benny said. "You go see your boss, and I'll go into the hospital and take care of the brothel inspector."

"We're supposed to be working together—"

"When we go after Adams we'll do it together," Benny said, "even though I think I can take care of him by myself. After all, we're in my backyard, not his, ain't we?"

"Benny," Cain said, "I really think we should both talk to Mr. Pemberton first."

"Cain," Benny said, putting his hand on the younger man's shoulder, "you can't go running to the boss every-time something comes up. You're gonna have to use your own common sense sometime, ain't ya?"

Benny was taking back control.

"I suppose . . ." Cain said.

"Let's divide up the labor," Benny said. "I'll take care of the brothel inspector, you do the girl—"

"All right," Cain said. "After that we can take care of Adams—but let's switch. I've been to the brothel twice already, and they know me."

"Fine," Benny said, "you go back to the hospital, and I'll take care of the whore. Then, if you want, we can go and talk to your boss about his daughter and Adams."

"He's your boss, too," Cain said.

"Yeah, right," Benny said. "Meet me later tonight at the graveyard."

"Benny—"

"Yeah, I know," Benny said, "you hate graveyards, but they calm me down. Let's make it eight. Okay?"

Cain sighed.

"Okay."

So much for young Cain's leadership abilities. Benny was disappointed in his young colleague, but maybe he'd be better once the action started. Or maybe he was simply a good bodyguard, and not much good for anything else.

Like real work.

Only time would tell . . .

Alicia had taken her buggy with her so Clint walked a while before he started looking for a cab. At one point he thought he was being followed, but when he turned around and took a look he saw nothing.

Alicia drove her buggy back to her house, wondering how she was going to explain being out all night to her father. Or maybe, since it wasn't Eric, he didn't even notice?

After he split from Cain, Benny decided not to follow Clint. Instead, he grabbed a cab immediately and gave the driver the address of the St. Louis Brothel Company.

He didn't know that Clint was going to the same place.

Cain went back to the hospital. All he needed was to find out what room the brothel inspector was in, then sneak in and take care of him. After that he and Benny could find out from Pemberton exactly what he wanted done with Adams, in light of the fact that there was apparently some sort of relationship between Clint Adams and Alicia Pemberton.

Cain thought if it was *that* kind of relationship—the kind he wanted to have with Alicia—then killing Clint Adams was going to be a pleasure.

THIRTY-EIGHT

Bertha liked the look of the big man—but then she always did like big men.

"What did you have a mind, big fella?" she asked. She led him into the sitting room, where all the girls were. She thought he'd want someone big and bosomy, and if she hadn't been just a few years past it . . .

"Her," the big man said, pointing.

Bertha looked where he was pointing and saw Jennifer, who had insisted on coming back to work.

"That's Jennifer," Bertha said. "Wonderful girl. Young and fresh . . . but I would think a little too . . . small for you?"

The man smiled.

"Like small women," he said.

"Hmm," Bertha said, "well, there's no accounting for taste, is there? Jennifer?"

Jennifer got up off the sofa and came walking over.

"Jennifer, dear, this man's name is . . ."

"Benny," the man offered.

"Why don't you take Benny up to your room and have him tell you what he wants, hmm?"

"All right, Bertha," Jennifer said. She took the man's hand. "Come on, Benny."

As Jennifer led Benny away he smiled back at Bertha and said, "Don't worry, I won't break her."

"Make sure you don't," Bertha said. "It would cost you extra."

Extra, Benny thought, for a hurt whore. How much extra, he wondered, was a dead one?

Clint's carriage dropped him in front of the St. Louis Brothel Company and the driver said, as Clint paid him, "Have a good time, sir."

"Thanks," Clint said. "I'll try."

He went up the steps as the carriage pulled away and knocked on the door. It was opened by Big Bertha, who was showing a lot of doughy cleavage today. She put her hand on her ample hip and raised an eyebrow at him.

"Come for your free one, this time?"

"I came to talk to Jennifer."

"That girl's been doin' more talkin' than anything, these days," Bertha complained. "You'll still have to pay."

"I just want to make sure she's safe," Clint said. "Jacob Webster is in the hospital."

"What happened?"

"Somebody gave him a beating yesterday, in an alley down the street from here."

"That's too bad," Bertha said, "but you're still gonna have to pay to talk to her."

Clint sighed and said," All right, I'll pay."

"Come on in, then," she said, backing away so he could enter—and that took a lot of backing.

"You'll have to wait a while, though," she said, after she closed the door. "She just went upstairs with a customer."

"She what? She's working?"

"Well, yeah," Bertha said. "She is a working girl, isn't she?"

"Who was the man?"

"I don't know," Bertha said. "A big bruiser, though. I thought he'd want someone a little bigger."

"Bertha," Clint said, starting for the stairs, "she could be in trouble. Someone almost beat Webster to death and she could be next."

"Honey," Bertha said, "she's just up there with a customer—"

"Damn it!" he swore, and started up the steps.

"Bubba!" Bertha yelled.

Before Clint could reach the top of the steps the big black man appeared there.

"You got to go back down, Mister," he said.

"Bubba," Clint said, "come with me to room four. I think Jennifer's in trouble again."

"Miss Jennifer? She's nice."

"And in trouble."

Bubba looked past Clint at Big Bertha, standing at the bottom of the steps with her hands on her hips.

"Make him come down, Bubba."

Bubba looked at Clint.

"I just want to knock on her door, Bubba, and make sure she's okay. You could come with me."

"Bubba!" Bertha shouted. "You hear me?"

Bubba turned sad eyes on Clint.

"I could lose my job, Mister," he said. "Sorry."

"Bubba, don't—" Clint said, as the big black man started down the steps toward him. Bubba was formidable, and Clint remembered that Cain had put the man through the front door. So Cain was more than formidable.

"Let's go, mister—" Bubba said, reaching out with huge hands when suddenly there was a scream from somewhere upstairs.

"Wha—" Bubba said.

"Bubba!" Bertha shouted.

"That's Jennifer!" Clint said.

Bubba turned and ran back with Clint close on his heels.

THIRTY-NINE

Clint saw Bubba hit the door, heard it splinter as he broke it down. Before he could reach the door, though, Bubba came flying back out. The big black man slammed into the wall opposite the door, and it, too, splintered. He hung there a moment, as if stuck to it, then slid down to the floor.

Poor guy just didn't seem too good at his job.

Clint went through the doorway into Jennifer's room. There was a big man there, bigger even than Bubba, and he had ahold of Jennifer by the neck with one hand. Her face was turning red, and would soon be darkening to blue if he didn't do something. Her feet were off the ground and she was kicking them.

"Uh-oh," the big man said. "It's the Gunsmith."

"You recognize me, huh?"

"Oh, sure," the man said. "I make a hobby of old West legends. I thought you wuz dead."

"Not yet," Clint said.

"Well, we can fix that," the man said, "soon as I finished with this little girl, here."

"You're gonna have to put her down," Clint said.

"Benny," the man said. "My name's Benny."

"You're going to have to put her down, Benny."

"Or what?"

151

"Or I'll have to shoot you."

Benny brought the hand holding Jennifer around in front of him. Jennifer hung down as if from the branch of an oak tree. Now she was between Clint and Benny.

"You gonna shoot me through her?"

"Why not?" Clint asked, sliding his gun from his holster. "If you're going to kill her anyway, what's the different?"

Benny frowned, because that made some kind of sense.

"On the other hand," Clint said, "you're a really big target, Benny, and she's a little girl. She doesn't make much of a shield for you, does she? I've got quite a few body parts to pick from. An elbow, a knee, one of those big tree trunks you call legs. I could hit you in two or three spots."

"Not before I snap her neck."

"Well, then we're back to square one," Clint said. "What's the difference if you kill her or I do? With me, it'll be faster, and then you'll be next."

Clint gave Benny a little time to think it over, but he couldn't give him too much, because Jennifer was running out of it.

"What do you say, Benny?" he asked. "How's this going to end?"

"You're gonna shoot me, anyway."

"Not so," Clint said. "If you let the girl go I'll let you walk out of here."

"Why would you do that?"

"Because it would be part of our negotiation," Clint said, "and that way nobody dies. I like that ending the best."

Benny wanted to think it over, but Clint could see that Jennifer had only a little time left.

"Now Benny," Clint snapped, pointing his gun.

Instead of simply releasing Jennifer, Benny threw her at Clint. He caught her with one arm, trying to keep Benny covered with the other one, but her weight striking him threw him off balance. He staggered back, his gun hand wavering, but holding onto the gun.

Benny charged him like a bull, slammed into both him

and Jennifer and three of then went out the door together, banging into Bubba, who was just getting up. They all went down in a heap. Jennifer rolled off Clint, but then Benny rolled onto him, groping for the gun. Clint tried to use his left elbow to fend him off, jamming it beneath the man's chin, but Benny was too big and strong. He knew if Benny got the gun they were all dead. Jennifer and Bubba seemed unable to help at all, so it was up to him.

Abruptly, he released the gun so that Benny would feel triumphant. The big man shouted his triumph and rolled off of Clint, but as he started to get to his feet Clint drew back both feet and lashed out, catching Benny in the face with both heels. His left heel struck the man's forehead, opening a wicked gash that sent blood streaming down, and his right heel mashed Benny's nose flat, sending blood into the man's mouth.

Blinded and choking, Benny amazingly still staggered to his feet, waving the gun.

"Stay down!" Clint shouted to Jennifer and Bubba, even though he had no idea if either of them was conscious.

Benny started pulling the trigger, his head and face crimson.

Clint, staying down, kicked out again, this time catching the big man in the knee. The leg bent the wrong way and buckled, and Benny fell to the floor. He reached out to catch himself, and in doing so released the gun. Clint scrambled for the weapon, grabbed it, then turned and brought it down on Benny's head. There was a sickening sound and the big man fell still.

"Is he dead?" a voice asked from the end of the hall. It was Bertha, and when Clint looked he saw that she and all the other whores in the house had been watching.

Winded, he said, "It would have been nice to have some help."

"That's what I hired Bubba for," she said.

Clint looked over at Bubba, who was just starting to sit up again. Jennifer was gasping for air still, holding her throat. Clint took a moment to consider Benny, whose head was lying at an odd angle on his shoulders. He then holstered the gun and went to Jennifer.

"Easy," he said, "take it easy." He held her and rubbed her back as she continued to gulp air. Then he looked down the hall and said, "I think this time you'll have to send for the police."

FORTY

By the time the police had removed Benny Doran's body—
they were *very* familiar with him—and had taken state-
ments from everyone involved, and determined that Jennifer didn't need to be hospitalized it was late in the day.

"Ma'am," one of the policeman asked Bertha, "why did
you let the man in if you weren't really open for business?"

"Well," she said, "he was big . . . I like big men."

The policeman—who was rather big, himself—retreated
at that point, and left.

Bertha stood outside Jennifer's room, looking at the
splintered door, and said, "I've had to buy too many new
doors." She turned and looked at Jennifer, who was standing next to Clint. "I'm sorry, Jennifer, but you're gonna
have to leave. I just can't afford to have you here, anymore."

"It's not her fault—" Clint started, but Jennifer cut him
off.

"That's okay," she said. "I was going to leave, anyway."

"I'll wait while you pack your things," Clint said. "Is
there someplace you can go.?"

"Maybe," Jennifer said. "I have one friend . . ."

• • •

155

After she packed they left and Clint discovered that the one friend she was talking about was Jacob Webster.

"He wants to travel west together, and I've decided to tell him yes," she said. "I decided he really means it when he says he just wants me to be happy."

That was when Clint had to tell her that Webster was in the hospital, having been beaten up the evening before.

"That must have been right after we got back," she said. "Did the same man do it who just tried to kill me?"

"No," Clint said, "I think it was the other man, the one who frightened you."

"And threatened me," she said. She had not told anyone this, until now. "He said I wouldn't be so pretty unless I told Eric Pemberton I didn't want to be with him."

That was ironic, Clint thought. Cain told her to reject Eric, and Pemberton was angry because a whore rejected his son.

"Can we go to the hospital?" she asked.

"Yes," Clint said, "I want to check on Jacob, anyway."

"He's the only man who ever really cared about me," she said. "I hope he's all right."

"So do I," Clint said. "So do I."

But he wasn't.

"I'm sorry," the doctor said, "but he's dead."

"What?"

"Oh, no!" Jennifer cried, bringing her hands up to her mouth.

"How did it happen?" Clint asked.

"Well . . . this is embarrassing," the doctor said. "The police have already been here. Apparently, someone got into his room and . . . murdered him."

"Cain!" Clint said, angrily. While Benny was trying to kill Jennifer, Cain had come here and killed Webster. Obviously, they would have come after him, next.

"Oh my God," Jennifer said. "Oh my God . . ."

And then she collapsed. Clint caught her before she hit the floor.

"Is she a relative?" the doctor asked.

"Yes," Clint lied. "His granddaughter."

"What are those marks on her neck?"

"Someone tried to strangle her earlier today."

"Someone tried to kill her, and also killed her grandfather?" the doctor asked, in disbelief.

"Yes," Clint said. "Doctor, he was her only relative, she has nowhere to go and I believe she needs medical attention."

"Say no more," the doctor said. "We'll admit her here and we won't charge her. It's the least we can do."

Clint silently agreed.

Later, when she awoke, Clint was sitting beside her bed. Beside him was Alicia, who had come to the hospital soon after Jennifer's collapse. She had not yet had time to tell Clint what happened when she went home.

"What happened?" Jennifer asked.

"You fainted," Clint said.

"Where am I?"

"You're in the hospital," he said. "They're going to keep you here for a while."

She stared at him for a moment, frowning as she fought to understand, and then she remembered.

"Oh, God," she said, "Jacob!"

Alicia put her arms around her while she cried, and then she either fell asleep or passed out. She eased her down onto the bed and they were chased from the room by a nurse.

"My God, what happened?" she asked.

"Let's sit down," Clint said, "and we can exchange stories."

FORTY-ONE

Clint told Alicia what happened when he got to the St. Louis Brothel Company, ending with Benny's body being removed and Bertha telling Jennifer she had to leave.

"That poor girl," Alicia said. "She left thinking she had one place to go, and now she has nothing."

"It's nice of you to feel sorry for her."

"Oh, I do," she said, "and in more ways than one."

"Which means?"

"Let me tell you what happened when I went home . . ."

As soon as she entered the house her father appeared and confronted her.

"Where have you been all night?"

"With a friend."

"What a friend?"

"Just a friend, Daddy. Why are you so upset?"

"I was worried about you."

"Why?" she asked. "I'm just the daughter. Nobody would ever think to kidnap me."

Her father looked puzzled.

"What does that mean?"

"Nothing," she replied. "It's just something I've wanted to say for a while."

159

"I don't understand you, Alicia—"

"I love you, Daddy," she said, cutting him off, "but there are a lot of things about you I don't understand."

"We're talking about you, young lady—"

"I know we are," she said.

"Stop interrupting me!" It was something he was not used to, and he didn't like it.

"Daddy, we have to talk."

"You're damned right we do," William Pemberton said. "I don't know what's happened to you, young lady, but I don't like it."

"I don't like it, either," she said, "but my eyes have been opened to a few things, Daddy, and I'd like to have them explained."

Pemberton narrowed his eyes.

"Who have you been talking to?" he demanded. "I don't have to explain anything to you."

"I've been talking to Clint Adams," she said, "and if you don't explain a few things to me I'm going to have no choice but to think the worst of you."

He glared at her, then said, "We better go into my office."

"What happened there?" Clint asked.

"We had a terrible fight," she said. "I asked about Eric, and Jennifer, and about you, and he refused to discuss any of it with me."

"Why?"

"Why? Because I'm a woman, that's why."

"That's never bothered you before."

"I've never admitted that it bothered me," she said, "but this is different. This is serious. People's lives are at stake and he thinks he has nothing to explain to me."

"So you left?"

"I stormed out," she said, "and said I wasn't coming back. I left all my belongings behind, too." She sighed. "I guess I'm in the same boat as that poor girl. Nowhere to go. And poor Mr. Webster . . . all he wanted to do was help that girl, and now he's dead."

"What about your brother?" Clint asked. "Did you see him?"

"No," she said. "If he was in the house and he heard us yelling he stayed away."

"Well, you can see him later, or tomorrow," Clint said. "Maybe he'll explain some things to you."

"Maybe," she said, "but I doubt it. He's just completely under my father's control, Clint. No, I'm just like Jennifer, now."

Clint didn't believe that for a minute and he felt sure that, in the light of morning, she'd realize it, too.

"You can go to my hotel and get some rest," he said. "You're welcome to my room for as long as you want."

"What are you going to do?"

"I'll stay here with Jennifer," he said. "I don't want to come back here tomorrow and find her dead, too."

"I'll stay with you," she said, "if that's all right?"

"That's fine, Alicia," he said. "Just fine."

William Pemberton was waiting when Cain Barrett walked in, still seething from his fight with Alicia. How dare she question him? Her, a woman, demanding explanations from him!

"What the hell is happening?" he demanded as Cain entered.

"The brothel inspector is dead."

"Who killed him?"

"I did."

"And where's Benny?"

"He went for the girl."

"And Adams?"

"We were going to go after him together, but first I thought you should know that we saw Alicia with Adams. She came out of his hotel with him this morning. It . . . looked like she spent the night."

"I know that!"

"You do?"

"She was here. We had a big fight. I want Adams dead, Cain. Where's Benny?"

"He went after the whore," Cain said, again. "She should be dead by now, too."

"You get ahold of Benny," Pemberton said, "and you finish Clint Adams . . . tonight!"

"I'm supposed to meet with Benny at the graveyard later on," Cain said.

"Find him before then!" Pemberton said. "I want this resolved tonight. I want things back to normal."

"Yes, sir," Cain said. "I'll find him and let him know."

"*Tell* him," Pemberton said. "I want it done tonight."

"Right."

"Well, get out and do it. Don't bother coming back until Clint Adams is dead."

FORTY-TWO

Cain couldn't find Benny anywhere. In the time the two had been standing across the street from Clint Adams's hotel they'd done a lot of talking, and Benny had told Cain about most of his haunts, but Cain couldn't find him at any of them, and he hadn't been seen, either. In the end Cain decided there were two options. Benny had killed the whore, and would be waiting for him at the graveyard, or something had happened to Benny and he wasn't going to show up, at all. That meant it was up to Cain to kill Clint Adams.

Seeing Alicia Pemberton coming out of Adams's hotel with him still stuck in Cain's craw. Killing him was still going to he a pleasure, even without Benny—he just had to figure out how to do it.

Eric Pemberton sat in his bedroom, wondering what the morning was going to bring. He had heard everything that had been said in the house that night. He'd heard the fight between his father and sister; he'd heard the words exchanged by his father and Cain. He knew that his father was condoning—no, demanding—the deaths of three people. And he knew that he was going to benefit from these deaths.

Something in him told him he should warn Jennifer, but after all she was just a whore. And the brothel inspector and Adams, they were just strangers. When they were all gone things would be just as his father wanted them . . . back to normal.

How could that be a bad thing?

Clint decided that the safest course of action was to stay right in Jennifer's room, and not sit out in the hall. He obtained the doctor's permission for this, so the nurses wouldn't constantly be trying to kick him out.

He and Alicia decided she should stay out in the hall. The both of them in the room with Jennifer might disturb the girl. When Clint grew stiff or restless he could come out and they could switch places. He'd be able to walk around the hall and stretch before they switched back.

During one switch—when Clint was coming out and Alicia was going in—she asked, "Do you really think they'll try anything at night?"

"Anyone who would kill a girl and an old man," Clint said, "would prefer the cover of night to try again."

"Do you think Cain knows what happened to this Benny fellow, and that Jennifer is still alive?"

"If he doesn't," Clint said, "then maybe we're wasting our time and he won't even come back here."

To Alicia, this didn't sound like the worst thing that could happen.

When Benny didn't show up at the graveyard after midnight Cain knew something was wrong. Could the big man have run into trouble at the whorehouse—maybe the big black man, or even Clint Adams, himself—and come out on the short end?

It was entirely possible.

By one A.M. he was convinced that Clint Adams was his to take care of—but where was he? At his hotel? Where else would he be? The hospital? The brothel inspector was already dead, so why would he be there? Unless Benny had hurt the girl before Adams had got to him.

Since he had orders not to come back until Adams was dead he decided that the lateness of the hour was not a deterrent. He'd go and check Clint Adams's hotel and, hopefully, find the man asleep in bed. If not, then he'd go and check the hospital. Maybe Adams had killed Benny, but Benny had put Adams in the hospital.

He knew one thing, though. If he found Adams in his hotel room, in bed *with* Alicia, it was going to be very hard for him not to kill both of them.

FORTY-THREE

It was four A.M. by the time Cain got to the hospital and saw Clint Adams in the lobby. By this time he was tired, annoyed, disappointed that he hadn't found the man asleep in his bed. He would have liked nothing better than to kill Clint in his sleep. After all, he was the reason that *he* wasn't asleep, right now.

Also, finding Adams in the hospital lobby meant it was likely the whore was in a hospital room somewhere. That meant that he still had to kill her when he was done with Adams.

Goddamn Benny, he thought. All talk. Big man and he couldn't back it up, couldn't kill a little whore. She would have been dead a long time ago if Cain's earlier orders had been to kill her, and not just to scare her.

He stood outside the hospital, staring into the well lit lobby, watching Clint Adams walk back and forth, and stretch. He was about to move in for a closer look when someone else appeared in the lobby, somebody he knew.

It was Alicia.

"How are you doing?" Alicia asked.

Clint moved close to her so no one could hear what he was saying but her. He gave her a few instructions, and

167

then sent her back into Jennifer's hospital room. After that he sat down on a bench in the lobby and waited.

Cain knew two things. One, if he killed Alicia he better leave Missouri because his boss would make sure he was dead. Two, he couldn't kill Alicia—not unless he had actually found her in bed with Clint Adams.

He moved closer to the hospital door to see if he could spot what room Alicia had come out of. She spoke briefly with Clint Adams, then turned and went back inside. He could not make out the room number, but he knew the location of the room, and that was good enough.

Cain moved around to the side of the hospital, took a moment to study it, and then picked a window. If he was right—and he thought he was—this was the room. The whore would be in there, and Alicia. All he had to do was wait until Alicia left again—he'd know that because the door would open, letting the light from the hall inside. Once she was out of the room he could force the window, get inside and kill the whore. If he couldn't force it he was sure he could break it, get off a shot and get away before anyone caught him.

But he wasn't going to run. They'd expect him to do that, but he was going to be too smart for them. He was only going to go around to the other side of the hospital, and he was going to wait for Clint Adams to come out, and then he'd take care of him, too.

But first, the girl.

He moved alongside the building until he reached the window he wanted, and then he peered inside. It was dark and he couldn't see a thing, but he still felt he had the right room. It wasn't hard to figure what window went with one door.

Sooner or later, Alicia would leave the room again. She'd have to, at some time. In fact, she might even switch places with Adams. If that happened he could get two shots off just as quick as one.

He took his gun from his shoulder holster, found himself a comfortable position, and settled down to wait.

FORTY-FOUR

Cain waited a good half-hour, and it was lucky he was a patient man. Finally, he was rewarded. There was some movement in the room and then the door opened. Bathed in the light from the hall was Alicia, very clearly illuminated. He waited just a few seconds to see if the door would open again, if Adams would come in. When that didn't happen he took out his knife and slipped it underneath the window. When he levered it up the window opened. He put the knife away, kept his gun in his hand, and opened the window wide. It didn't make a sound. He paused to listen, didn't hear anything, and then climbed inside. Once he was in his tired brain kicked in and he realized three things.

First, the window had opened too easily.

Two, when he paused to listen he should have heard the breathing of someone who was asleep, and he hadn't;

Three, he was dead.

Clint gave Cain time to climb in the window. As he did so the man was backlit by the moonlight, the same moonlight that had enabled Clint to notice the man when he was in front of the hospital.

The bed was empty, Jennifer having already been removed from the room while Cain was working his way to the window. Alicia was out of the room, having successfully stood in the light long enough to be identified.

Clint was on the other side of the bed, gun in hand, waiting for Cain to come in the window—which he did.

Clint stood up and said, "Right there, Cain."

Cain froze, and didn't panic. Clint had the feeling that the young man had realized his mistake as soon as he entered the room,. It was all just too damned easy for him not to.

"Adams?"

"That's right."

"And the girl?"

"She's gone."

"You saw me."

"Yep."

"Shit."

"It doesn't have to end badly, Cain."

"Can't end any other way," Cain said. "I can't leave unless you're dead."

"Or unless you are."

Although Cain was certainly more visible than Clint was, Clint knew that the other man was stalling, hoping that his eyes would become accustomed to the darkness in the room. He could give him enough time for that.

"Benny?" Cain asked.

"Dead, Cain," Clint said. "Like you if you don't drop your gun."

Now or never, Clint thought—and Cain thought the same thing.

"Okay, Adams you win—" Cain said, and lifted his gun.

Stupid, Clint thought, even as he fired. As smart as they were in life, just before they died most men had the stupidest moments of their life. This man was no different.

The bullet struck him dead center. He grunted and staggered back, tried to lift his gun again. Clint fired a second shot. It hit Cain high in the chest and took him out the window.

Clint rushed the window, because if the two shots had not killed the man he's probably be on the run. When he got to the window, however, he saw that the second shot had done the job. Cain was lying on the ground under the window, dead. His gun had fallen from his hand and the moonlight glinted off of it as it lay several feet away. Silver-plated. Fancy, Clint thought.

The door to the room opened and Alicia came in. She propped the door open. A nurse came in behind her and lit the wall lamp. Alicia walked to Clint's side and looked out the window. The room was brightly lit now, and so was Cain as he lay on the ground.

"My father sent him."

"No doubt," Clint said. "He said he couldn't leave unless I was dead, like those were his orders."

"Orders," she said, shaking her head. "It's a good thing you spotted him when you did, or Jennifer might be dead. Or you."

Clint ejected the spent shell from his gun, let it drop to the ground next to the dead man, fed a live one back in and holstered the gun.

"What now?" Alicia asked.

"Now we go and see your father," Clint said, "and make sure it's over."

FORTY-FIVE

Alicia still had her key and used it to let herself and Clint into the Pemberton house.

"Go upstairs and get your brother," he said. "I'll get your father and take him to his office."

She had already told Clint that her father's bedroom was downstairs, while hers and her brother's was on the second floor.

"Clint . . . don't . . ."

"Don't what?"

"Kill him."

"I don't want to kill him, Alicia," Clint said. "I want to make sure he leaves Jennifer alone."

"I just—"

"Get Eric and bring him down," Clint said. "He should see this."

"All right."

He crept down the hall to William Pemberton's bedroom. When he reached it the door was open, a lamp was lit, and the room was empty. He looked further down the hall and saw another light. Apparently, the man was already in his office, either because he couldn't sleep, or because he had work to do.

Clint walked the rest of the way down the hall and entered the office. Pemberton was seated at his desk, chair turned to the side, wearing a silk robe. He had the chair pushed back and kneeling between his legs was a blonde woman, her head bobbing up and down on his lap.

"Yes, yes," he was saying, with his head back, "this is what I need to relax me."

"You're going to need a lot more than that, Pemberton," Clint said.

Pemberton's eyes opened and he stared at Clint in disbelief. The girl, intent on what she was doing, did not know anything was wrong.

"What the hell—" Pemberton said, and pushed the girl off him as if she was an annoyance. "What the hell are you doing here?"

"Are you a whore?" he asked the girl, who was now sitting on her bare ass on the floor. She had amazingly small breasts, barely bumps, and was so thin he could see her ribs.

"Yes."

"Pay her off and let her go, Pemberton," Clint said. "You won't want her to hear any of this."

"Who do you think—"

"Do it quickly, man. Your daughter's in the house. Do you want her to see this?"

Abruptly, Pemberton opened a desk drawer, took out some money and threw it at the whore.

"Get dressed and get out—fast!"

She scrambled to her feet with the money clutched in her hands, grabbed her clothes and ran past Clint, still naked. Hopefully, she'd pause to put her clothes on before she ran outside.

Pemberton rearranged his robe to cover himself, then turned his chair so that he was facing Clint.

"What is this about?"

"Your men are dead."

"My men?"

"Benny and Cain."

"You killed Cain?"

"That's right."

"And the girl?"

"She's still alive."

"But the brothel inspector is dead."

"That's right," Clint said, "and he's the one you have to pay for."

"Nonsense," Pemberton said, waving a hand.

"The girl will be leaving," Clint said. "You don't have to worry about her. I'll be leaving, as well."

"Then I have nothing to worry about."

"Yes," Clint said, "you do."

"What?"

"You have to worry about them."

He turned toward the door. Alicia took her cue and entered with her sleepy-looking brother, who was also wearing a silk robe.

"What's going on, Father?" Eric asked.

"Nothing, Eric," Pemberton said. "Go back to bed."

"Eric is staying, Daddy."

Pemberton looked at his daughter.

"You have betrayed me."

"I kept you from having a young girl killed," Alicia said. "I can't believe you'd do that."

"You don't understand business."

"No, I don't," she said. "It's because I'm a girl, right? A daughter? Not a son?"

"Eric understands."

She looked at her brother.

"Do you?" she asked. "You understand murder?"

Eric looked at her helplessly for a few moments, then looked at his father.

"He believes and understands what I tell him to," Pemberton said.

"As I used to, Daddy," Alicia said, "but no more. You had a man killed, and tried to have a young girl killed, and

for what? Business? You'll have to explain that to someone."

"To who?" he asked. "The police?"

"Yes."

"And who's going to tell them?" Pemberton asked.
"Him? A stranger in town? Or that girl? A whore?"

"No," Alicia said, "not them. Me."

"No . . . you won't," Pemberton said, as if he couldn't
believe it.

"Yes, I will." She looked at her brother. "Come with me,
Eric. Come with me to the police."

"You can't do that, Alicia," Eric said. "You can't."

"Come with me."

"I can't," he said. "I-I'm getting married next month."

"You see, Alicia?" Pemberton said. "You'll have to go
alone."

"I will, Daddy," she said. "I'll go, and I'll tell them."

"Go ahead," Pemberton said. "They won't do anything."

"Why not?" she asked. "Because you own them?"

Pemberton looked at Clint.

"Are you going to kill me?"

"No," Clint said. "For your daughter's sake, no."

"Then leave the city, and take the girl," Pemberton said.
"I won't try to stop you, or find you. As far as I'm concerned, it's over."

"That's big of you, Pemberton," Clint said. "Real big."

Clint looked at Alicia.

"I'm coming with you," she said to him. "Take me to
the police."

"Alicia—" Eric started, but his father cut him off.

"Let her go, Eric," he said. "No one will believe her, and
if they do, they won't do anything about it."

"I feel sorry for you, Daddy," Alicia said.

"Don't, little girl," he said. "Feel sorry for yourself."

"Come on, Clint," she said, and stalked out of the office.

Pemberton looked at Clint and said, "She'll be back."

Clint shook his head, turned and left.

•   •   •

Outside Alicia asked, "Is he right, Clint?"

"About what?"

"About the police?"

"He probably is," Clint said. "You were right, inside. He probably does own them."

"So then he gets away with murder?"

"And builds your brother a political career on the bodies."

"If it wasn't for me, would you stop him?"

"No."

Watch for

END OF THE TRAIL

220th novel in the exciting GUNSMITH series
from Jove

Coming in April!